Praise for *Other Broken Things*

"This book is a blinding beauty."

—Martha Brockenbrough,
author of *The Game of Love and Death*

"Desir crafts a portrait of a teenage
alcoholic that is honest and unsparing."

—*Booklist*

"Fans of A. S. King, Laurie Halse Anderson,
and John Green will appreciate this gritty, honest
portrayal of the road to recovery."

—*VOYA*

"Natalie's story is told without judgment
and with an uncanny understanding of
the twelve-step program. . . . This title deserves
a place on high-school shelves."

—*School Library Journal*

Also by C. Desir

Fault Line

Bleed Like Me

Love Blind
(with Jolene Perry)

BOYS
ALONE
HIGHER POWER
RESILIENT
FEARLESS
MORAL INVENTORY
FIERCE
MORE THAN OUR SCARS
BOOZE
RELATIONSHIPS
SPONSOR
SOBER
REHAB
ADMIT
DENIAL
PUNCH
TOO FAR
DRUNK
LOVE
BELIEVE
SERVE
ALL HONESTY
TATTOOS
NOTHING
HOLIDAYS
BOTTOM
ROCK

OTHER BROKEN THINGS

BY C. DESIR

OBSESS
ADDICTION

Simon Pulse

New York London Toronto Sydney New Delhi

SIMON PULSE

An imprint of Simon & Schuster Children's Publishing Division

1230 Avenue of the Americas, New York, New York 10020

First Simon Pulse paperback edition April 2017

Text copyright © 2016 by Christa Desir

Cover illustration copyright © 2016 by Dave Foster

Also available in a Simon Pulse hardcover edition.

For information about special discounts for bulk purchases, please contact Simon & Schuster Special Sales at 1-866-506-1949 or business@simonandschuster.com.

The Simon & Schuster Speakers Bureau can bring authors to your live event. For more information or to book an event contact the Simon & Schuster Speakers Bureau at 1-866-248-3049 or visit our website at www.simonspeakers.com.

Cover designed by Jessica Handelman

Interior designed by Tom Daly

The text of this book was set in Weiss Std.

Manufactured in the United States of America

2 4 6 8 10 9 7 5 3 1

This book has been cataloged with the Library of Congress.

ISBN 978-1-4814-3739-4 (hc)

ISBN 978-1-4814-3740-0 (pbk)

ISBN 978-1-4814-3741-7 (eBook)

To Julio, love of my life.

And to Asher, who helped me find my way out of this book.

Chapter
One

I'd cut a bitch for a cigarette right now. Unfortunately, I'm sandwiched in the car between inflatable Santa and inflatable Frosty and the only person within striking distance is my mom.

"You sure you don't want me to come in?" she asks as she tugs at her hand-knitted red-and-green striped hat. Mom is the mascot of the holiday season. Pretty sure she pees eggnog and her armpit odor is peppermint scented.

"It's a closed meeting, Mom. I told you that. Only the alkies get to go. Not their moms. Plus you've got to finish decorating."

My fingers curl in and out of my palm. Someone at the meeting has to have a smoke. *Has to.*

"I was looking online. There are some open meetings in the city. I could go with you to those."

I wave my hand. "Mom. Stop. I'll be fine. I went to a meeting every day in rehab. I know the drill. Pick me up in an hour."

I shove Frosty to the side and push open the backseat door. Yes, I'm in the back. Like a toddler. The passenger seat has been taken up by inflatable Rudolph. I slide out and Mom turns down "Feliz Navidad" long enough to call out to me.

"Proud of you, Natalie. You've got this."

I wave again, resisting the urge to give her the finger, and turn away so she doesn't see my eye roll. Mom's obviously fit time in her busy holiday schedule to read some of the *Big Book*— Alcoholics Anonymous's bible to getting my shitty life together, told through a series of steps and stories of pathetic losers just like me. Jesus.

The brown building in front of me is nondescript with the letters SFC on a plaque in front. As I step up to the door, my hands shake a little. Not from the DT's—you need to be way deeper down the rabbit hole than I ever got for delirium tremens—but from the whole business of it.

AA meetings are a requirement. Three times a week until I'm three months sober and then twice a week until I'm six months. Six months feels like for-fucking-ever at this point, but honestly, a month ago, six hours felt the same.

I pause outside the door and stare at the sign taped to the front. Meeting times, plus a plug about movie nights and a Sunday-morning pancake breakfast. There are three meetings every day. I can't imagine going to that many meetings in a day. What the hell for? How many times does someone need to hear the Serenity Prayer?

I slide my hand in my coat pocket and finger the card inside. *Go in, zone out, get your card signed.* Drawing in a deep breath, I push through the entrance and am immediately hit by the smell of BO and burned coffee. I blink my eyes a few times to adjust to the light and see I'm in a hallway. A door on my right says FELLOWSHIP MEETING ROOM.

Another breath, this time through my mouth so I don't have to deal with the BO stench. My heart is beating pretty hard. Even more than the first time I got in the boxing ring, a million years ago when I thought things were different.

There's a long mirror on the side of the door, like we somehow might feel the need to check our appearance before going in to confess our drunken transgressions. My ridiculously curly hair is pulled back neatly in a band, my slapdash makeup job is miraculously holding up from this morning, and the rest of me looks Abercrombie solid. This is definitely my 12-step best, so I'm not sure why I'm stalling.

Somehow, walking into a meeting room felt easier at rehab. Probably because I had a nurse escorting me. I squeeze my eyes shut and grip the knob, pulling open the door. Wishing with everything I have for this not to be real.

The room smells too. Different, though. Like musty books and defeat. Yes, defeat has a smell. A distinct cigarette smell, with zero traces of alcohol. An old woman near the door looks up and smiles a little at me. A quick scan around the room shows three black dudes in conversation around the big table, an obviously drunk or hungover Hispanic dude with his head leaned against the back wall, and a white guy talking to a woman with red hair and a scowl on her face. The white guy looks up when I enter and nods at me.

No beaming smiles or welcoming committee here. No one's happy to see me. They're all dealing with the same shit. I'm another soldier who's been drafted into the army of addiction. Hardly cause to celebrate. On the plus side, from the look of things, there's no way anyone here is going to be digging that deep into my business, which means I won't have to think— something I've gotten excellent at in the past month.

I unwind the scarf at my neck—hand-knitted by Mom, of course—and plop into a chair at the table. A quick glance at the clock shows I have five minutes before the meeting starts. I need to time this better. Or bring cigarettes next time so I can smoke beforehand. But I finished my last one this morning, sitting on my window ledge and watching Mom hang icicle lights. She frowned when she saw the cigarette, but didn't say anything. She's been on me about them since I got back, but she must have figured a lecture about them would have been less than welcome this morning.

The red-haired lady stands up from the table and approaches me. Ah. Meeting leader. I know by now talking to the newbies is part of their job.

"Kathy," she says, sitting in the plastic chair next to me. "First meeting?"

"First meeting here. Not first meeting ever," I mumble in response. Wonder if I could get her to sign my card now and then leave the meeting early. I give her a long look and realize she's not the type to break rules. She's got that hard-living look about her, and if she's a meeting leader, she's been in AA awhile now.

"Got a sponsor?" she asks.

"No. I'm just out of rehab."

She nods and I catch the white guy watching us. Not even slyly. Just openly staring. I have an urge to flip him off, but I doubt it'll earn me any brownie points and I have a card I need filled up.

"Take out your phone," Kathy says. I pull out my cell and she snatches it from my hand like she's going to confiscate it. Instead she presses some buttons and hands it back to me. "I'm in your contacts now. Call whenever."

"Natalie," I say.

She nods again and gets up. "Find a sponsor, Natalie. You're too young to be in here."

I almost roll my eyes, but that'd just be proving her point. I am too young. Seventeen. Way too young for rehab. Way too young for AA. It's all sort of bullshit, but to say my parents are overprotective is an understatement. So here I am. Two days out of rehab, two months after a DUI, surrounded by people who don't know anything about me, with a court card in my pocket, and wanting to beat the crap out of just about everyone.

Happy fucking holidays.

Chapter
Two

"**This is the twelve thirty** closed meeting of the Stevenson Fellowship Center. The only requirement for attendance is a desire to stop drinking. Calvin, can you please read 'How It Works'?"

I look at my Uggs and let the drone of Calvin's voice wash over me. I've heard the "How It Works" speech dozens of times. I could practically recite it in my sleep. And Calvin is a mumbler so it's not like I could understand him anyway. I want to shut my eyes like the Hispanic guy in the back. His mouth has dropped open slightly and he's either passed out or he's fallen asleep. For the hundredth time I think how I don't belong here.

Driving was stupid. I get that. But I wasn't plastered. I've been way drunker, and frankly, the whole thing would've been fine if I hadn't hit wet road. And if I hadn't been distracted by the shit show of my life. The "legally drunk" thing is sort of bullshit. You hit your legal limit after one drink. I've seen people have way more than that and be perfectly fine driving home. It's all a scam between insurance companies and the government to squeeze more money out of the working class. I'm not saying people should drive loaded, but seriously, three drinks is hardly shit-faced, despite what a Breathalyzer might say.

The topic for the meeting is the Second Step: *Came to believe that a Power greater than ourselves could restore us to sanity.* Cue zone-out time. The higher power thing is a really big part of AA. At first I got into all sorts of arguments in rehab about how scientifically, God just isn't possible, but I quickly realized that wasn't getting me any closer to being released or convincing my therapist that I'm fine. So now I tune it out and nod when other people talk about their spiritual awakening as if it isn't all a big fat crock.

As the three black guys drone on about getting right with God, I examine the room. The main wall behind Kathy has huge signs on either side of the door. The Twelve Steps on the left, the Twelve Traditions on the right. I still haven't exactly figured out the Twelve Traditions. Seems like it was sort of slotted into the program so people didn't turn AA into a moneymaking organization. Fools.

The rest of the room is brown paneling and bookshelves filled with self-help books and framed pictures of guys who were presumably important to the AA organization. I don't have the first fucking clue who any of them are, though I guess one must be Bill W. The giant clock on the wall draws my attention and I count seconds along with it as the old woman who smiled at me when I walked in starts to talk about medication and the Good Lord. Fifteen, sixteen, seventeen, eighteen . . .

The room has gone quiet and I look up to see everyone staring at me. Crap. I blush a little as the white guy shifts forward in his chair and drops his hands on the table.

"My name is Natalie, and I'm an alcoholic."—"Hi, Natalie."— "Grateful to be here today. I think I'd prefer just to listen." I've said this more than a dozen times over the last month. It's a mantra as much as anything else in my life. And it gets me out of having to share anything. I couldn't do it all the time in rehab, because my therapist sort of caught on to it, but I did it as much as I could.

The white guy has tats on his knuckles. I notice the letters of *KILL* on the left one. And some weird symbols on the right one. This is unexpected, as the rest of him looks pretty clean-cut. As clean-cut as you can look in AA. Jeans without holes. Flannel button-down over a long-sleeve white tee. Clean-shaven. Blond hair that isn't too long or shaggy. If I had beer goggles on, I might say he's a Bradley Cooper look-alike. And no dark shadows under his eyes. He's been sober awhile, I'm guessing.

The rest of the meeting carries on, but I don't listen to anyone. There's a thin strip of windows above the bookshelf and I mostly stare out at the gray sky. In the end Kathy lets us go early—which never happened in rehab—because no one else has anything to say. We circle up and I find myself holding hands with the white guy—Joe, I think—as we say the Lord's Prayer together.

My gaze stays too long on the *KILL* on his knuckles as the group chants, "Keep coming back. It works if you work it . . . sober." Everyone else has let go of each other and started to disperse.

"Can I get my hand back?" Joe says, and I drop it like I've been burned. God. What the hell is wrong with me?

"Nice tat," I say with a smirk.

He nods. "Saving up to get it removed. Or get a new one put on top."

I wrap my scarf around my neck. "Trying to get your outsides to match your insides?"

He shakes his head in this way that reads like he's disappointed in me. Not sure what the fuck for, as I haven't done anything as far as he knows. "Dry drunk?"

"Huh? What's that?"

"You know . . . the people working the program because they have to. Sober because someone told them to get that way. The ones who relapse the fastest."

My mouth drops open. "Fuck off, dude. You don't know anything about me."

Kathy comes over then and nudges Joe. "Leave Natalie alone. She's here. That's what matters."

He shakes his head again and zips up his coat. "I'm going out for a smoke. I'll see you."

"Yeah. You coming to breakfast on Sunday?" Kathy asks.

"Nah. Can't. Gotta do a work thing. You'll need to cover

it." He trains his eyes on me and for a second I think I see concern. But it's masked right away into indifference. "Come back, Natalie. Even if you don't believe it. It might sink in eventually."

I nod and shove my hands in my pockets. I finger the court card and wait for him to leave, but he lingers just long enough that I get pissed and pull out the card anyway. He's fucking with me and I frankly don't care. I push the card at Kathy. He scoffs and heads out the door, muttering.

"Can you sign my court card?"

To her credit, she doesn't even bat an eye. "DUI?" she asks.

"Yeah. Like I said, I'm just out of rehab. Now I've got six months of meetings and community service."

She grabs a pen from the basket full of two-dollar donations and signs the card. "Rehab your parents' idea?"

"Yeah."

She hands the card back to me. "You're lucky."

"Hardly."

"Least you got someone who gives a shit enough to help you get sober."

So, huh. Kathy isn't going to treat me like a kid. Maybe she's my ticket out of this place.

"Well, that might be overstating things," I say.

She shrugs. "Your folks drive you here?"

"Yeah."

"There you go then."

I almost tell her I don't really fit here. I almost tell her I'm not an alcoholic. I almost tell her this is all bullshit, but I decide against it. For some people all this stuff means something. They become addicted to meetings in the same way they became addicted to booze or drugs in the first place. I saw a ton of kids in rehab on their third go-around who were all gung ho about meetings, and it didn't take me long to realize it was just replacing one thing with another. Therapy and group became their new drugs.

Personally, I'd take booze over sharing bullshit feelings any day, but who am I to burst someone's bubble? So I nod at Kathy and thank her and tell her I'll see her again.

"You got my number. Use it," she says to my back as I'm walking out.

"Sure thing," I call to her.

I pull out my phone and delete her contact info before I'm through the front door.

Chapter
Three

Of course Joe is the only one outside smoking. What a worthless group of alkies, not one of them even hangs out to smoke. I release a breath and take a step forward. Before I can pull my shit together enough to ask to bum a cigarette, Joe thrusts out his pack and flips the lid open.

"Thanks," I say, and grab two Parliaments, hoping he doesn't see me slide the second one into my palm.

"Could've just asked for two."

My shoulders drop. This is the problem with sober people. They're so fucking observant. I hold the second cigarette out to him, but he shakes his head.

"Keep it."

"Thanks." I put one of the cigarettes in my mouth and lean into the lighter he's held up, taking a deep drag. I was only ever really a social smoker before, at parties or after I was stoned or when I was drunk and tired and needed to stay up. Now cigarettes are my candy canes. Delicious and something I want all the time.

"Sorry I gave you a tough time," he says. I inhale deeply and hold the smoke in my lungs until it burns the back of my throat.

"Whatever."

"What's the court card for? DUI?"

"You all must see a lot of those."

He shrugs. "When teenagers are in here it's almost always because they got caught by the cops. Sometimes it's just open bottles in their cars, sometimes it's DUIs."

"How come you guessed DUI for me?"

He takes a drag from his cigarette and lets out a long stream of smoke. "'Cause you don't look like a kid who got caught being stupid just once."

I flick my ash at him, but he doesn't even step back. "What do I look like?"

"You look like a kid who's done a bunch of stupid shit and it finally caught up to her. You look like an addict."

I take two full inhalations before I piece together a response in my head. "First, I'm not a kid, period. Second, I'm nothing like any of those people in there. I've said four sentences to you. What do you know about my life?"

He drops his cigarette and steps on the butt. Then he picks it up and tucks it back in the pack like he's going to dispose of it later in the proper canister. Do-gooder. Should've figured.

"I don't know anything about it. But I've been coming here for over five years. I've seen dozens of you come and go."

I blink. "You've been sober for five years and you're still coming here?"

He shakes his head. "Only sober for three of them. The first two I was just dicking around, trying to figure my shit out after being locked up."

Whoa. So maybe not such a do-gooder.

My head is spinning. This dude actually has a backstory. I can almost ignore all the Judgy McJudgyPants parts now that I know he's been in prison. "What were you locked up for?"

"What were you in rehab for?"

"Driving drunk."

He nods. "Me too."

I take a last drag on my cigarette and then crush it on the ground. His gaze darts between my face and the cigarette. After a few seconds he sighs and leans down to pick it up and tuck it into the box with his. Heh. Sucker.

"That must not have been your first DUI if they locked you up," I say.

"It was. But it wasn't your standard DUI."

"Jesus. Did you hit someone? Kill a biker or something?" I want to take a step back, which is ridiculous and wimpy, but somehow it feels a little too real for me, a thing I've been patently avoiding, so maybe I don't want to be having this conversation.

Joe shakes his head. "No. I drove into a White Hen Pantry, shattered the front window. Then I panicked and bailed. DUI. Leaving the scene of the crime. An unsympathetic judge.

It all added up to a few months in corrections."

"Fuck, dude. You shattered a window and left the scene? You must've been really loaded."

He shrugs. "It was a long time ago."

I think about lighting up the second cigarette, just so I can get more of his story, but I see Mom's Lexus pull onto the street. Great.

"I gotta go," I say. And now I feel like a child because my mom's here to pick me up. Like I'm on a playdate, not cruising out of the twelve thirty AA meeting.

He nods. "I hope I see you again, Natalie."

I shrug. Maybe he will and maybe he won't. Probably depends on him more than me, since I'm going to be here on the regular for at least a few more months. I give him an awkward wave and bolt to my mom's car. I'm not sure why, but suddenly I feel way younger than I have in years. Like some dude just schooled me, even though he really didn't.

Mom's bursting with questions when I slide in—the front passenger seat this time, Rudolph is evidently safely at home—but I hold a hand up and shake my head. Then I roll down the window, search through my jeans pockets for my lighter, and light up the other Parliament that Joe gave me.

"In the car, Natalie? Really? Is this smoking thing *that* necessary?"

"Well, Mom, you pick, cigarettes or all the other stuff I've been up to this past year? Your call."

Mom's mouth drops into a tight frown, but I know she's not going to say anything. She wants to talk, but not if she can't steer the conversation. She's careful that way, not liking to get her hands too dirty if she can help it. Which frankly suits me just fine. She turns up the Christmas music and starts humming as I blow smoke into the frozen air.

One meeting down, fifty-nine to go.

Chapter
Four

I'm not even sure why I'm bothering with catching up at school. I'm a senior. This is supposed to be my coast year. Only my grades suck. They sucked last year too. I'll either end up at a shitty state school or community college, if I graduate this year at all. A month away at rehab is a long time, and to be honest, I was pretty much phoning it in most of the semester, most of the past year really, so the rehab excuse is pretty flimsy. I'm going to have a crap ton of incompletes, but I guess it's better than failing. I don't care about school, but I do care about getting out.

Luckily, I only have three weeks until winter break. Most of my teachers are actually being kind of cool about the stuff they're piling on, trying to minimize the assignments I don't really need to do. I'd be shocked by it if I didn't know it was all motivated by my mom meeting with each of them when I was in rehab, discussing my "situation."

My first day back, my ex Brent comes up behind me at my locker and slides his hands so they're less than an inch below my boobs. Classy. Can't believe how much time I wasted with this guy.

"Fuck off." I slap his hands and turn to see a shit-eating grin on his face.

"Nat. I missed you. How was rehab?"

I shrug. "How the hell do you think rehab was? It's rehab. Not Universal Studios. And I wouldn't have even had to go if I weren't driving your drunk ass home."

He steps forward and grabs my belt loops, pulling me into him. Brent is hot, but he's a huge player and I'm not in any kind of place to deal with our past crap. "That's not how I heard it. I heard you got in a wreck three blocks from your house. Smashed into a stop sign. That's not my fault."

Okay. That's probably true. The fact of the matter is that I would've stayed at the party way longer and gotten a lot more hammered if he weren't puking in the bathroom and I hadn't felt obligated to take him home. Not that he deserved it, but he's held my hair enough times for me to return the favor.

"Still. It was after I dropped you off, so it's partly your fault. And I don't see your parents sending you to rehab, even though you must've gotten grounded for being so wrecked that night."

He slips his thumbs under the hem of my shirt and for a second I remember how good he is with his hands. Really good.

But I don't need this noise, so I push him off and turn back to my locker.

"I told them I was burning off steam. Stressed out about college applications. They let me off," he says. Of course they did. His parents are *those* kind of parents. The kind that want to be cool. Don't get me wrong, I'd kill to have parents like that, but still, it's all phony bullshit.

A bunch of people pass behind us, but they ignore us. Our school is pretty big. Close to five hundred kids in each class. Not really the kind of place where you pay attention to what's going on outside your circle of friends.

Brent presses up against me from behind and rests his hand flat on my stomach. He drops his face into my neck and sucks a little on my skin. It's been too long since I've been touched, I think.

"Are we having a moment here?" I snap, shaking myself out of the urge to sink back into him.

"I missed you," he says, and something in his voice sounds real. I turn and he's dropped the player mask and looks like he wants to talk.

Hell no. I've worked too hard to forget Brent and the whole mess of him in rehab.

"No you didn't. You probably had your tongue down some girl's throat fourteen seconds after I was admitted to the hospital."

He bristles, but it shuts him down. "Don't be a bitch."

I shrug. "Calling it like I see it."

His face changes again and I can almost hear him calculating. The way his face works, he's the loudest thinker. I wait to see how he's going to play this, ready to shut him down again.

"Wanna go somewhere and spark up?" he asks.

Unexpected. For a second I consider it, but then he steps forward and slides his hands around my hips, circling his thumbs against my stomach, and just like that, I jab him in the gut.

"Jesus," he hisses. "What the hell was that for?"

I grab my Coach bag, not even sure I've put all the right books in there, but it doesn't matter because I need to get away from this. "Brent. I can't get high with you. My parents made me go to rehab. They're having me pee in a cup every week. They're jury-rigging the car with an attachment that will keep it from starting unless I do a sober Breathalyzer. So the answer is no. I'm not going to spark up with you. I don't even like you."

He shakes his head. "You used to like me."

"No. Not really. I used to like fucking you. I never actually liked you."

He looks hurt for half a second, but then he snaps back. "Such a pretty mouth. You can still fuck me. I don't care if you like me."

I let out a long breath and hitch my bag on my shoulder. "Yeah. I'm gonna pass. But thanks for the offer."

"Nat . . . ," he calls as I barrel down the hall.

I turn, see his face, and immediately regret it.

"We should talk." All pretenses are gone now. His expression is hard and serious.

I flip him off. "Nope. Save it for your therapist." Then I swivel on my heel and bolt down the hall as fast as I can go without breaking into a run. I clench and unclench my fists, using the physical sensation to block out everything. Move forward, don't look back, don't think, don't feel. I used to have booze to help with this, but now I only have my brain's refusal to hang on to anything from before rehab. Which luckily, is enough.

On my way out I see my American history teacher, Mrs. Hunt. Crap.

"Natalie, you haven't completed any of your outstanding assignments."

A gaggle of girls passes behind me, whispering, and I'm almost positive I hear the word "lush." I take a step closer to Mrs. Hunt and drop my voice.

"I don't know if my mom talked to you about where I've been for the last month. But I wasn't exactly in a place to be doing assignments."

Mrs. Hunt's face is cold and unsympathetic. "Your mom did talk to me. She talked to *all* of us. And I did agree to make an exception to my homework policy for you because of your *medical* issues. But I emailed your assignments to you a few days ago. I assumed I'd have received at least one of your incompletes by now."

She's a bitch. And has no idea what I'm going through. But I'm not about to let her know she's getting to me. So I smile sweetly and say, "Of course, Mrs. Hunt. I'll have two to you by tomorrow."

She doesn't return my smile, just nods and heads down the hall.

I slam out the double doors and dig in my bag for my cigarettes, soft leather rubbing against my fingers as I search. We're not allowed to smoke on school property, but the minute I hit the street, I'm lighting up. Most of the smokers hang out in a courtyard by the strip mall, but I'm not friends with any of them and I'm not super interested in chatting at this point.

A car pulls up alongside me on the sidewalk and I peer in. Amy and Amanda. My "friends."

"Are your parents still making you go to AA?" Amy says, leaning out the window. Her hair is flat-iron perfect, but I can see from her eyes that she's already pretty wasted. This is what we do. What I did. Water bottles full of booze to get us through the day.

"The court is, actually."

Amanda snorts from beside her. Neither of them should be driving, but that's never stopped us before. Amanda even took her driving test buzzed. We all thought it was hilarious.

"It's not the same without you, Nattie," Amy says.

I shrug. "My mom talked to all my teachers. They're paying extra attention to me. I can't pull off the stuff I used to."

And frankly, I'm tired and don't really want to. Being with

Amy and Amanda requires too much energy. They're always looking to me for entertainment and it's exhausting. I'm an awesome drunk, but since getting out of rehab, I haven't reached out to them. I've wanted to drink, but not with them. Not with anyone, really.

I never understood the alcoholics who drank alone, but watching Amy and Amanda shove each other and bust into uncontrollable snorts of laughter over nothing makes me totally get it. I want to be alone more than anything right now. The reminder of Brent's fingers and his mouth on my neck and the look on his face and the *We should talk*, it's pinging around inside my brain and all I can think about is making it go away. And not with the likes of Amy and Amanda.

"I gotta go," I say, and smash my cigarette butt on the ground. I consider picking it up, but that's stupid. Frickin' Joe.

I turn to leave and Amy calls out, "When are you done with it all? When do we get you back?"

I shrug and don't say what I'm thinking, which is: *I don't want to go back to either of you.*

When I get home Mom is in the midst of a cookie-baking frenzy. The kitchen is covered in racks of cookies and cookie tins. Her short blond hair is sticking straight up like she hasn't even had the chance to shower. Which, no way, nothing would keep Mom from showering. What if someone were to drop by?

I grab three of those peanut butter cookies with the Hershey's kiss on top and beeline for my room. If I spend any more time in the kitchen, I'll wolf down at least a dozen of them. I'm not so great with the stopping mechanism. But I've got other plans. I have twenty minutes until I have to leave for the afternoon AA meeting and that's probably just enough time.

I lock myself in the bathroom in the hallway and pull open the medicine cabinets. Downstairs I hear Christmas music piping into all the rooms. God love techie Dad and his plan to create the perfect home for entertaining. I set aside boxes of tampons and Ace bandages until I finally find the bottle I'm looking for.

Tylenol with codeine. Thank Christ for getting my wisdom teeth out a year ago and leaving half the bottle intact. I probably would've hit this way sooner, but it's been so easy to get booze or pot from people at school. Now I don't want to bother with the hassle of that. I just need numbness for a little while. I don't have the first clue how much of this will do the trick, but after the day I've had, I'm going toe up.

I finish the bottle in three long swigs and chase it down with a glass of water and a thorough teeth brushing. By the time Mom calls me down to leave for the meeting, I'm already feeling the effects. I hold myself as steady as I can and walk downstairs slowly. Concern is etched on her face.

"Are you okay?"

I nod. "Exhausted. There's a lot to catch up on at school. Don't really have time for this meeting."

Her mouth pinches. "You're going. Not negotiable. If you need more time to catch up at school, I'll talk to your teachers again."

I wave my hand. My fingers feel swollen and fat, like they used to when I'd bare fist on the punching bag. "Not necessary." It might be necessary, but I'm not quite lucid enough to discuss it at this time.

I pull my coat, the knit scarf, and a hat on and examine myself in the hall mirror. Tylenol aside, I look better than I have in a while. Over the past year, I'd gotten really thin and not in a smoking-hot way, more in a chemo patient way. I'd lost all my muscle tone. My therapist in rehab said it was the booze, though it could've been not entering the gym for months. I blink slowly. My cheeks are a bit flushed and I could probably retouch my makeup, but my limbs feel like they're moving through sludge so I leave it.

I follow Mom into the garage, concentrating very hard on my steps, one foot in front of the other. So hard that I don't even notice my car is parked there. Fixed.

Mom beams at me. "Early Christmas present. We know how hard you've been working the program. So we got it fixed. And the Breathalyzer is hooked up. Dad did it. It was almost like one of his tech projects."

I snort. "Almost."

The garage is starting to spin and I brace myself against the door of Mom's Lexus.

"You can drive yourself today," she says.

I yawn. "If you don't mind and it doesn't mess up your cookie schedule, I'd like you to drive. I'm pretty tired and I don't want to fall asleep at the wheel."

Her gaze narrows for just a second and I steel my face into an expressionless mask. She won't ask, I'm almost positive. She hasn't asked about anything, not since the hospital, and even then, it was all vague inquiries as to how I was feeling. Old habits die hard. She smiles at me, pure plastic, and locks down any questions she might have. "I don't mind taking you. We can listen to Christmas music in the car."

Fucking perfect.

Chapter
Five

Shit. Damn it to hell. Joe's at the meeting. An afternoon meeting. I thought he was a noon-on-Saturday guy. He's been sober three years. Why does he hit up more than one meeting a week? Jesus fucking Christ, I don't need this.

I slink to the back of the room when I enter, dropping myself into the same chair the Hispanic guy sat in during the first meeting. I shut my eyes for less than a minute, or three, and feel a body slide in right next to me. I don't even need to crack an eye to know it's Joe. He smells like Parliaments.

"What are you on?" he asks in a low voice.

I peel my lids open and blink at him. "What? What are you talking about?"

He shakes his head. "Your speech is too clear for you to be drunk. What'd you take?"

"Nothing. Fuck off."

He leans in. "Tell me what you took or I'll tell Blake over there not to sign your card."

Crap. I got a Boy Scout on my back now. Spectacular. "Tylenol. I had a headache."

He shakes his head and stands up, taking a step toward Blake, who is apparently in charge of the four o'clock Wednesday meetings. I grab Joe's hand and pull him back down.

"It might've had some codeine in it."

"Jesus, Natalie. What are you doing to yourself?"

I'm too fuzzy to get into this with him, so I decide on "Not sure why this is your business."

He swears under his breath and settles in next to me as Blake starts the meeting. Every time I start to feel myself dozing off, Joe elbows me in the ribs. Today's meeting requires each of us to read aloud from the *Big Book*, but the words are way too blurry for me. I try to pull the "I'm just going to listen today" line, but it sounds dumb because it's not like I've been asked to share my own words, just Bill W.'s.

"Natalie can't read," Joe says.

I shoot half-assed daggers at him with my eyes, but he lifts a shoulder and reads my part for me. When the book has gone around the room and Blake has given everyone a chance to comment—there are only two other people in the room besides us, a woman who looks like a soccer mom and one of the black dudes who isn't Calvin—we circle up, hold hands, and recite the Lord's Prayer again. Joe's hand feels rough and my fingers tingle at the touch. Tylenol with codeine is pretty awesome, as it turns out.

Joe drops my hand before we even finish saying "It works if you work it . . . sober" and steers me back into the corner. I pull out my court card to give to Blake, but Joe snatches it and tells Blake he'll take care of it. When the room completely clears, I turn on him.

"You better sign that. I need it or I'll have to do more community service."

"What community service are you doing?"

I look at my feet. They're kind of swirly and distracting and I forget Joe's question until he tips my chin up with his two fingers and repeats himself.

"Oh. I thought I'd volunteer to wrap presents at the bookstore. The proceeds go to this children's literacy thing."

He shakes his head. "No. You're not wrapping presents. That's rich-people community service."

"Fuck off. I can do any kind of community service I want."

He sighs. "Jesus. No wonder you're such a mess. Do you always get what you want?"

"That's legit community service."

Joe's eyes are dark brown, which is weird because his hair is blond. His eyes are pretty, I think, and his lashes are super long, and I sort of wonder how old he is. He has wrinkles, but not like my dad.

"What are you looking at?" he says. Crap. Okay, Tylenol with codeine is maybe not so awesome.

"How old are you?"

"Older than you."

I stick my tongue out and he actually laughs at me. "Seriously, Joe. How old are you?"

"Thirty-eight."

"Dude. That's old. That's like me. Times two. Plus . . . four."

He snorts. "Good math, tiger. Now, just so you know, the judge isn't going to let you get away with wrapping presents as community service. Trust me on this one. I tried every BS trick in the book. They're not forgiving on DUIs."

Huh. So it's not quite the same as our school service project then. Those are so bullshit that last year one of the kids passed out flyers for his dad's photography studio and the school counted it as community service.

"What do you suggest?"

"Work the pancake breakfasts here on Sundays."

I squinch my face up. "I don't think so. This place smells and I can only imagine what it's like when you add pancakes and bacon to that mix."

"Such a princess."

"Bite me."

"Natalie . . . ," he starts, and I can already hear the paternalistic concern. Which, no.

"What are you even doing here, Joe? You're *sober*. For three frickin' years. Surely you've memorized the steps by now. Gotten right with the Lord. Given it up to your higher power.

Taken your fearless moral inventory and laid all your shit bare to some other poor soul."

"Well, look at that, haven't had so much codeine that you can't mouth off still."

"Honestly. What do you want?" The room is getting clearer now and I'm kind of pissed at how much Joe is interfering with my buzz. I have an uncontrollable urge to uppercut him, but my hands don't want to make fists quite yet.

"You're a brat. You don't know the first thing about this program. Plus you showed up here high. I'm not signing your card."

I snatch it from him and move to leave. I don't need this crap. I'll have to go to the six thirty a.m. meeting tomorrow to make up for it, but whatever. I'm done listening to Joe.

"Natalie," he calls as I stomp out.

"What?" I glare and almost expect him to laugh in my face, but instead his gaze softens.

"You think I haven't been there? You think I haven't done everything I could to make it all go away? Tylenol with codeine? That's nothing. Try nail polish remover. There's alcohol in that, you know. Cough syrup. Mouth wash. Windex, for Christ's sake. You think you're badass. You're what, seventeen? You have no idea how low you can sink from this disease. You're lucky you caught it so early."

I'm stunned silent. I can't imagine. Windex? Surely that could kill you.

"I'm not your problem," I whisper.

He nods. "Yeah. Still." He approaches me slowly, tugging his wallet from his back pocket. He slips out a card. "That's me. Cell phone's on the back. Call if you need help. There's a woman's group at St. Paul's Church on Friday nights. You can probably find a sponsor there. Until then, call me if you start thinking Tylenol's a good idea again."

Chapter
Six

I get home and go right to bed. Sleep through dinner. Wake up so dehydrated my skin feels like it's going to crack off. It's five o'clock in the frickin' morning and even though I feel like complete crap, all I can think about is how a quick swig of vodka would do me a world of good right now.

I drag myself out of bed, and because no one's up yet, I drop down and do a hundred sit-ups and push-ups. I'm completely winded by the time I'm done, but at least I did them. So some of the me from long ago is still in there somewhere. I consider heading downstairs to our workout room, having a go at the punching bag, but I can't. The idea of it is too defeating, and opening the door to that means stirring up a whole mess of other crap I don't want to deal with. Instead I stand under the shower way too long, moving my hands over my ribs, my hips, my stomach. I keep my mind intentionally blank, refusing to think of all the things my body's been through.

Then I straighten my hair, which takes forever, and pick out clothes that hide my newly increasing ass. Maybe chemo patient skinny wasn't so bad. I stare at the homework I didn't do last night and decide I'm still not in any kind of shape to pull that off. I'll have to go to the nurse during American history. Instead I boot up my computer and block Brent from all social media. I've got to move forward if I'm going to make it through these next six months, not get waylaid by a bunch of "we should talk" pleas from that handsy fucker.

By the time I head down for breakfast, I'm at least at 50 percent, which all things considered is a goddamn miracle. Mom is at the stove, making chocolate chip pancakes. Our kitchen is massive, with stainless steel appliances and marble countertops. It opens into both the living room and the dining room, the perfect hub for a house built to host banker dickheads and their insipid wives.

We used to have parties for Dad's work clients all the time. I had my first drink when I was eleven at one of their parties. Usually the holiday season means different "couple" friends at our house every Saturday, Dad telling boring work stories and Mom flitting about making sure everyone's glasses and plates are filled. Then we have the big neighborhood party on the day before Christmas Eve.

When I got out of rehab, Mom told me she and Dad canceled all this season's hosting obligations, including the big neighborhood one. I still don't know if it was for my benefit or if they were worried I was too much of a loose cannon around their friends. And of course, Mom didn't explain.

"You must be starving," she says now. I try not to notice the Mrs. Claus stitched on her sweatshirt, but it's impossible. Mrs. Claus has a ruffled skirt sewed on that when you lift it up shows her mistletoe-covered bloomers. Mom is sadly oblivious to how hilarious it is that Mrs. Claus is requesting kisses underneath her skirt.

"Yeah. I could eat," I answer.

"I guess you really were exhausted?" It's a question. As if she thinks I'm going to come clean about something. Though the truth is I'm pretty sure she wouldn't want me coming clean about shit if it meant really talking.

"I told you I was."

I grab the milk from the fridge and pour a big glass of it. It's cool and delicious when it hits my throat. That's a weird thing about being sober: food and drink actually taste really incredible. I've put on at least five pounds since I quit drinking, and that's even with crappy rehab food. I can't imagine what kind of havoc the gluttony of Mom's holiday season is going to wreak on my body. Push-ups and sit-ups have little chance against chocolate pumpkin loaf and sugar cookies.

I swallow the rest of the milk along with my guilt about not spending any time at the gym. Not that that's even an option for me, but still. If I shut my eyes, I can smell it: the tape on my hands, the sweat, the blood. I shake the thoughts from my head and drop into a seat at the breakfast table.

She slides a plate in front of me. "You have an appointment with Dr. Warner today."

I'd completely forgotten, and relief washes through me. I'm not going to even have to fake sick for Mrs. Hunt. For as much as therapy is a huge pain in my ass, Dr. Warner only sees patients between nine and noon, so I miss school. He's a prestigious psychiatrist who teaches at the hospital university in the afternoon. I don't have the first clue why he even wanted to take on my little problem, but my parents have money and I'm guessing that accounts for a lot.

"Dad already gone?"

"Of course," Mom says, plucking dried poinsettia leaves off the centerpiece.

Dad works at the Board of Trade. He's gone most days by five. He's super disciplined about his whole life. Church on Sunday. Gym every day after work. He runs marathons still. And is überefficient. I'm sure a fuckup like me for a kid is a raging disappointment. He hasn't said as much, but it's not like he's driving me to AA meetings or reading the *Big Book* either.

"There's a women's meeting at St. Paul's tomorrow night." I can't believe I said that. The last thing I want to do is go to another meeting. At the same time, my damn card only has one signature on it so far, and I'm not super psyched about the idea of getting extra community service just because I can't manage to sit through a few hundred "if you want what we have . . ." lectures.

"Women only?" Mom's eyebrows are practically at her hairline. She's no idiot. She doesn't know who, but she knows at least part of the source of my problems is because of a dude. Fricking Brent.

"Yeah. Maybe I'll find a sponsor there."

She beams like I've informed her there really is a Santa Claus. My poor mom somehow has taken this whole thing on her shoulders, and I do feel a bit bad about it. I've told her in a million ways that I'm fine, but the accident and the DUI and the hospital were a pretty big deal to her. She pretends they weren't, but you can't really fake not being anxious. At least, not that well.

"That would be great," she says. "Finish your breakfast and I'll take you to Dr. Warner's."

I'm pushing it, but I can't help blurting out, "Maybe I could drive myself. Test out the new Breathalyzer."

Shit. Tylenol wouldn't show up on that, would it? Momentary panic is replaced by the annoyed voice in my head telling me I'm being a freak and I need to man up already.

"Well," Mom says, fussing with her already perfect hair, "I need to do some errands downtown anyway. And I thought I'd kill two birds with one stone. And Dr. Warner may want to talk to me afterward."

Ah. She wants to make sure I don't sabotage the piss test. The things she doesn't say are almost louder than what she does. Mom's about as subtle as Mrs. Claus with mistletoe on her ass.

* * *

The piss test is clean. Apparently codeine doesn't show up on the test, or else they weren't screening for it. File that one away under clandestine ways to get high. Dr. Warner is stodgy and methodical, and doesn't seem to mind that I eat all the butterscotch candies on his desk as he talks to me. I'm pretty sure he thinks the whole therapy thing is bunk because he keeps trying to push antianxiety meds on me. I originally suggested Xanax—which can be popped like Tic Tacs if you want a mellow buzz—but Warner was absolutely against it because they're super addictive. Heh. Go figure.

Mom talks to him for five minutes afterward and puts her foot down about the whole medication idea. She thinks kids are overmedicated and should be able to make their lives stress-free on their own with fruitcakes and caroling or some shit. Dr. Warner tries the patronizing *little lady* thing on her, but Mom doesn't fall for it. She's gotten that crap from Dad for years and she can smell an amateur mansplainer like Warner a mile away.

So no meds. Another appointment made for two weeks from today. And Mom's assurance that I'll keep going to AA meetings. I leave his posh office, which looks more like a law firm than a psychiatrist's office, and smile to myself over the idea of Mrs. Hunt getting her panties all twisted up when she sees my empty desk.

* * *

I make it to school in time for lunch. I grab a plate of fries and a bunch of ketchup packs and scan the cafeteria. I could sit with Amy and Amanda, but I'd rather have teeth pulled than watch them sip from their water bottles and slur-whisper about how wasted they are. I've got to get new friends.

Brent raises his hand and pats the seat next to him, but I roll my eyes and head for the smoker table instead, same place I've been sitting for the past few days. They're all burnouts, but at least they don't really say anything. Stoners can be pleasantly quiet and I sort of wish I'd picked that as my drug of choice instead of vodka.

"What's up?" they say when I sit down.

"Nothing," I answer, and that's pretty much all that's required of me for the rest of the meal. It's even better than an "I'm just going to listen" meeting.

The cafeteria monitor watches me like a hawk the whole time, but I don't care. I finish my fries and then fish out my history notebook, half-assing an assignment for Mrs. Hunt. I'm dying for a cigarette, but I don't think I can sneak out of school when I just got back. Instead I pull out a full pack of Big Red and chew piece after piece until the bell rings. Amy and Amanda stumble past me toward the exit and don't say anything.

On my way out of the caf, I bump into Camille. My best friend from junior high. A lifetime ago. We lost touch a few months into high school, me spending all my time at the gym and her hitting the honors track pretty hard.

"Heard you were in rehab?" she says. Not mean, more curious.

"Yep," I answer, shouldering my bag.

"You're sober, then?" Her beautiful, tan face is makeup-free and serious. Camille has always been a serious girl. When we were in fourth grade, she told me she wanted to be a corporate lawyer. She wasn't even fucking around or making it up. She'd researched it.

"Totally sober," I answer, swallowing down the guilt over the Tylenol. Camille doesn't know shit about me anymore.

"Are you going to go back to boxing?" She tucks her black hair behind both ears. She wears her backpack on both shoulders so her hands are always free. It's a weird thing, and maybe only someone who's used to fighting would notice, but she's done it forever. Not for quick blocking protection, though; she does it so she can talk with her hands.

"No."

Her hands come out now in a big gesture, fingers twirling around each other. "Well, it's not my business, but you were better then."

Anger whips up my spine, making me throw my shoulders back. I'm done with this conversation. "Thanks for the feedback, Camille, but you're right. It's not your business. Later."

The day drags on and more than once I pull out my phone and Joe's card, but then tuck both away again. One honest conversation hardly makes us besties. But the mundaneness of school pelts at me, and keeping my head down and doing my work takes an obscene amount of energy.

I take off after my last class and realize I have nowhere to be and nothing to do. Once upon a time I had friends like Camille who were normal. But I got caught up in stuff. Stopped returning calls, stopped going out with them, became friends with guys at the gym. Only to lose all of them too. Then it was just me and Amy and Amanda and Brent and the casual acquaintances who lost to me at beer pong on the weekends.

I pause outside of school and look at my phone. Three thirty. My drinking friends are undoubtedly five miles past buzzed and well on their way to hammered. Which leaves . . . basically no one.

For a second the loneliness of the day and the shittiness of my circumstances hit me like an unexpected left hook, winding me and making me drop to the curb by the bus stop, my legs sprawled out and the cold ground seeping through my pants. This time I don't think too hard, but pull out my phone and Joe's card and thumb in his number.

"What are you doing?" I say before he even gets a hello out.

"Working. What are you doing?"

"Not a goddamn thing. It's weird. I'm not sure what to do with myself." God. Was that too honest? I hate that my voice sounds needy. I do not want to need this guy.

"Well, Natalie, you could go to a meeting."

I laugh. "Fuck that. Meetings aren't the answer to loneliness."

"Loneliness? Are you . . . ?"

"I'm not going to a meeting, Joe."

"Meetings help with loneliness."

"Oh, Joe, is that where you've met all your BFFs? I can only imagine the rocking time you all have together, chips, cards, and Diet Cokes on a Friday night."

"I could do a lot worse. So could you."

I'm about to say there's nothing worse, when I see Amanda and Amy stumble into the parking lot. They head toward the gym across the street and I already know what the next hour is going to look like for them. The gym has a pool and it's easy to sneak up to the spectator seating and finish off a flask while giggling at all the guys in Speedos. I was the one who first brought them there.

"Natalie?"

"Yeah, I'm here."

"What's wrong?"

"Nothing. I just called you because I'm bored and you don't appear to do much."

He laughs. "What's that supposed to mean?"

"Four o'clock meeting on a Wednesday? Do you work banker hours, Joe?"

"Depends on the day. And you appear to have quite a bit of free time too. Didn't you just get out of rehab? Surely you have some schoolwork to catch up on."

"Only if you can come over and play tutor." The loneliness of a few minutes ago is fading with the idea of messing with Joe.

"Pass. Thanks for the offer, though."

Jesus. This guy. It's like he is incapable of flirting. Or maybe too old for it. "Are you sure, Joe? I think I can rustle up Catholic schoolgirl knee-highs and a white button-down."

"I'll bet. So. There's a meeting in twenty minutes. You could probably make it."

"Enough. You're such a bummer. Fucking impossible. Do your boy parts even work?"

He laughs hard and now I'm feeling very pleased with myself. "You need to find a hobby."

And just like that, I feel like crap again. I'm a yo-yo of emotions and it sucks. "No hobbies. I had a hobby. I don't have it anymore."

"I'm not talking about bar hopping. I'm talking about doing something real that you're passionate about."

I shake my head, swallowing past the boxing-glove-sized lump in my throat, and consider hanging up on Joe, but then it occurs to me that he doesn't know. I'm new to him and everything in my history is a blank slate.

"I *do* need to find a hobby. How about sexting?"

"Oh Jesus. You're a mess. Go to the meeting or go home. I need to get back to work."

I grin wide because I've flustered him, which is exactly where I like guys to be. "Bye, Joe."

"Bye, Natalie. Be careful."

I snort and then click End.

❋ ❋ ❋

Friday, I leave for the women's meeting early because I'm so fucking excited to be driving my car again. Even if I did have to breathe into a tube to get the thing started. Jesus, technology. I circle the block six times, and probably would keep driving but my practically blank court card is shaming me from inside my coat pocket.

The church fellowship room is packed. None of this six-people-at-SFC bullshit; there are at least forty women in the room. My "I'm just going to listen" speech is going to be cake in this crowd. I may not even need it. Probably you have to raise your hand to share.

I'm settling in, clutching my card in my pocket, trying to figure out which of the women standing by the coffee machine is the leader, when Kathy slides in next to me.

"Natalie, right?"

I nod.

"Give me your phone." She holds out her hand and I blink at her.

"What for?"

"Just give it to me."

I pull it out and hand it to her. She types in a bunch of numbers and hands it back. "That's me. Again. You'll probably delete it, again. I did that too when I first came. A lot. My sponsor gave me her number four times before I didn't lose it on purpose."

Oh.

I tilt my head and look at her hard. I used to intimidate opponents in the boxing ring with it, but Kathy doesn't even blink. Just raises both eyebrows and looks at me like she could block any attack I'd make, left-handed. I sort of like Kathy. She's crusty and her skin is complete shit. Like pockmarks from picking at acne and huge pores clogged up with grease and dirt. But still, she's kind of real. And I think she might be a natural redhead.

I don't even know what I'm doing, but Dr. Warner told me that by my next appointment I had to have a sponsor so I mumble, "Will you be my sponsor?"

"What?"

I sigh and try again. "Will you be my sponsor?"

She blinks. "Huh. That's unexpected."

I shrug. "Why? Everyone says go to meetings, get a sponsor, stay sober. That's how it works, right?"

She nods. "I know how it works. I'm just surprised you were ballsy enough to ask me. I figured you'd be one of the types to avoid it. Think you could get better on your own."

I can get better on my own. I'm not even sick, but I've had *that* conversation enough in rehab to know it leads nowhere. So I raise a shoulder and say, "I don't really want to put it all on my mom. We're supposed to work the program with someone who's been through it, right?"

Kathy looks at me thoughtfully and I know I've got her. "Yeah. Your mom's not a good person to be accountable for you. That's really yours to own. But you can't do it alone. So. Okay. We can try it. Meet me at the Starbucks on Seventh and Main, Sunday morning at nine, okay? We'll go over some rules."

Rules? Jesus. The whole thing feels a little like asking a guy to prom and then finding out you have to coordinate your dress with his tux color and figure out the limo and everything else, and I sort of want to puke from it. But it's done. Dr. Warner will be happy, Mom will be happy, Joe will be happy. Not that I'll see that dude again, probably. But still. If I do, I got something to throw back in his face when he pulls that "you think I don't know what it's like" BS.

The women's meeting is way lively. And by the end I realize I'm dealing with a bunch of girlfriends at a sorority house. Even the way they complain about their husbands and kids is sort of hilarious and has nothing to do with being drunks. Mom would probably love this meeting. It's like a stitch 'n bitch of teetotalers. The whole thing makes me antsy—the lack of real girlfriends in my life is painfully obvious every time these ladies mention hanging out together—and I probably would've slipped out to smoke and only come back for the last five minutes of the meeting if Kathy weren't sitting next to me, providing commentary on every single woman talking.

"She only looks that good because her husband's a plastic surgeon.

"That one comes every week declaring her years of sobriety

and I've seen her coming out of the liquor store at least three times in the last six months.

"She's only going to AA because she doesn't want to deal with her anorexia."

I have to bite the inside of my cheek to keep myself from laughing. Kathy, it turns out, is an asshole. And evidently not totally focused on her own sobriety, what with the gossip she's got on pretty much everyone. Assholes, I know how to deal with. At the end of the meeting, as she's signing my court card, I hand her a piece of paper with my cell number on it.

"Look at you," she says, folding the paper and tucking it in the outside pocket of her shitty pleather purse. "This might work out after all."

Chapter
Seven

Brent texts me on my way home Friday night, asking if I want to meet at Amanda's.

You don't have to drink. We can just fuck around, he adds. Charmer. Like that hasn't gotten me in a world of trouble before.

Apparently he hasn't figured out yet that I've dropped him from my circle. I consider texting him back a few choice words, or blocking his number altogether, but frankly I don't give a shit enough to do either. Instead I pull out Joe's card and call him up.

"I got a sponsor," I say smugly.

"I already heard."

"What? Jesus. What the hell? Is my name in some database somewhere? I thought AA was anonymous. You fuckers are so full of shit."

He chuckles. "Relax, tiger. Kathy called me."

So maybe they're a thing? "Are you dating?"

He laughs again. "Nah. Nothing like that. She's way too much woman for a guy like me."

"Am I too much woman?"

He cough-chokes. "Are you flirting with me?"

I smile inside my dark car. "I don't know. Do you have any cigarettes?" Because yes, I'm out of them again.

He laughs. "I always have cigarettes. I can't figure out why you don't. Your parents are rich, right?"

"Oh my fucking God. Have you done a background check on me?"

"Hardly. I saw your mom pick you up in a Lexus. I'm guessing you can't get one of those on layaway."

I snort. "What even is layaway? Is that an old-guy thing?"

This is all strangely comfortable and I'm not sure what to make of that. I'm not creeped out by it. If I'm being perfectly honest, I've fucked around with dudes I've had less conversation with. Maybe Joe is some kind of father figure; my sober way of working through daddy abandonment issues.

"I'm at the O'Hare Oasis. If you feel like talking and smoking, have your mom drop you off here."

My stomach swoops a little, butterflies taking off in a mad frenzy. So I guess not daddy issues, then.

I grin. "I'll have you know, thanks to my dad's handy-dandy car-starting Breathalyzer, I'm driving my own wheels. So I'll see you in fifteen."

I click off the line and slide my phone into my coat pocket. I trace my finger along the edge of the business card Joe gave me. Geothermal heating-and-cooling specialist. What the hell is that? I drop his card back into my purse and smile to myself a little. I've never messed around with an older guy before.

Chapter
Eight

My phone is going crazy with texts as I pull into the oasis. I've ignored them for the past fifteen minutes because I don't need to get back on the cops' radar with a ticket for texting and driving. Plus that shit's not safe.

I park and pull out my phone. A passive-aggressive text from Mom. *Just checking if the meeting's over yet?* And three booty call texts from Brent, plus one more saying, *You owe me a conversation, Nat.* Whatever.

I text Mom back. *Meeting is done. Having some fellowship time with some of the women here. Found a sponsor. Be home in an hour or two. Don't worry, the Breathalyzer still works on the car.*

She texts back a smiley face, a Christmas tree, and two Santa emoticons. And *I'm* the one with the problem.

The O'Hare Oasis is like a megamall of shitty food joints. Joe is sitting at a table outside Popeyes with two biscuits on a plate in front of him. I slide into the chair across from him and snatch a biscuit.

"Why, yes, Natalie, I did buy those for you. You're welcome."

I smile at him. "They wouldn't be sitting here if they weren't for me. These biscuits are addictive. I'm surprised you resisted the temptation of devouring them yourself. You must really like me."

He pulls off his baseball cap and sets it and a pack of Parliaments on the table. "Actually, I can't figure out what I think of you yet."

"I find the quickest way for people to get a read on me is to get me naked. It clears up a lot of confusion."

I'm in my element here. This, I know how to do. Guys are such suckers for girls who talk dirty. I don't mean really dirty, just enough to tease them into thinking you're into them.

Only, Joe doesn't react how most guys do. "Natalie. What is it you're trying to accomplish here? I'm not going to sleep with you, if that's what you're hoping. And I'm not going to enable you. So what do you want?"

Huh. "You don't want to sleep with me?"

"I'm thirty-eight."

I smirk. "That's not an answer. Plus you're kind of hot for thirty-eight, and you look a whole lot better than most of those dried-out alkies."

"Do you know anything about AA?"

"It works if you work it."

He rolls his eyes and I can almost see what he would've looked like at my age. Fewer wrinkles around the eyes, less stubble, whiter teeth. But he is still hot and the idea of kissing him isn't one of my worst.

"When you were in rehab, how far did you get in the Twelve Steps?" he asks, flipping the box of Parliaments over and over.

"Well, they fast-track you in there, you know? So I'm at like Eleven."

His gaze bores into me. "Step Eleven? Really?"

I pick up the second biscuit and take a small bite, licking my fingers afterward and watching him for a reaction. Nada. "Are you gay?"

He grabs my wrist and I drop the biscuit. Whoa. Kind of strong. "I'm not gay. I'm not getting involved with a teenager. Stop licking your hands. Stop trying to mess with me. It will *not* work."

"Sheesh. Okay then."

We sit in silence for a few minutes, until it is painfully awkward, so I pop up and grab my purse. "This has been . . . whatever. So, I guess I'll see you, Joe."

And because I can and because I'm sort of pissed, I snatch his box of Parliaments and shove them in my purse before heading out.

"Step Four, Natalie. Go back to Step Four," he calls after me.

I lift my hand over my head without looking back and flip him off. *Step Four: Made a searching and fearless moral inventory of ourselves.* Step Four, my ass.

❋ ❋ ❋

Brent is waiting outside my house when I get home. Fucking great.

"What's your problem, Nat?" he says as I lock my car door and take a step toward the house. He steps in front of me, steering me halfway down the block and into his car.

When he gets in the driver's side, I turn to him with a bland expression. "I thought I made myself clear the other day."

"Well, *I* thought we had a thing. An arrangement or whatever." He's pouting. I can't believe I ever thought this guy was hot. He's like a little boy.

"You mean when I get hammered, then suck you off? That stellar arrangement?"

He actually has the balls to blush. "It wasn't only about that."

"Yeah. It kind of was. And frankly, the novelty of it wore off when I got sober."

He shakes his head. "Don't pull that shit on me. You're sober *now*. I guarantee next year, next month probably, you'll be back to partying. It's who you are. And I, for one, don't mind that girl. I don't want you to be anyone else. I take you one hundred percent at face value."

"Well, that is a thing, I guess. But you know, B, I'm not sure *I* liked that girl."

This is actually the truth. It wasn't just feeling like shit hungover or needing a water bottle full of orange juice and vodka to make it through my classes. It was everything. It was sort of a project, partying all the time. An exhausting project. I miss the numbness of drinking pretty fierce, but I don't miss the BS drama around it. The constant figuring out how to drink more, how to slip past my parents unnoticed, how to get home from a kegger when everyone was too loaded to drive. Or the endless texts from Amy and Amanda about whose parents were gone and who has a fake ID. It was all more a pain in the ass than anything.

And surprise, surprise, I got out of rehab and no one really gives a shit about me anyway. Except my Christmas Nazi mom. And Brent, who wants to rehash a bunch of shit. My friends are people who got loaded with me, and when I came back with a court card and a piss test requirement, I've become less fun to them. They're around still, and they wouldn't care if I hung out with them, as long as I didn't kill their buzz.

But Brent's trying and I feel kind of bad about him now. I touch his cheek and he leans forward to kiss me but I stop him. "You're not a complete prick. I just can't get back into it with you, you know?"

He slides his hand around the nape of my neck and pulls me forward. "Why not? We've got *history*. I don't care if you're sober or drunk. I'll take you as you are."

I pull back. I so don't want to get into our history. "Yeah. I know. I get it. But the truth is, I can't be with someone like that. Fucking AA. I'm not supposed to be with anyone at all until I'm a year sober. But even though I don't give a shit about that, I still can't be with someone who parties. It's too hard, you know?"

I hate the itchy feeling on my skin. I hate the uncomfortability of truth. But I owe it to Brent, especially because I refuse to give him anything else. The least I can do is offer him part of an explanation.

"I could've loved you," he whispers, and now I do roll my eyes and push him away.

"Don't be stupid. Save that shit for someone who's going to fall for it. Maybe Lizzie. She's always been sort of into you."

He shrugs. "Not my type. I like girls with curly hair and big mouths."

He wags his eyebrows and I swat him, then pull the car door open. "Get over it, B. Virgins are people too. And maybe she's saving herself for you." I slam the door shut and trudge back to my house, wondering if I should call Joe to apologize.

Before I figure it out, my phone pings in my purse. I pull it out when I get to my front porch. Text from Joe's number.

You should head over to the pancake breakfast after you meet with Kathy on Sunday.

I add his name to my contacts and text back.

You going?

The front door opens and Mom looks at me anxiously. "What are you doing out here?"

I hold up my phone. "Making plans with one of my AA buddies."

She ushers me in and fusses over hanging my coat as I read Joe's return text.

It's not a date, Natalie. But I'll hook you up to start working the break-fast if you're interested in fulfilling your community service.

I smirk and can't help typing back, *I knew we weren't done with our hooking-up conversation.*

Mom is watching me, but I don't even care. I stare at my phone and wait for his response. It comes thirty seconds later.

Brat. ☺

Chapter
Nine

Brent texts me again on Saturday morning, because he's either stupid or tenacious. And I'm actually starting to wonder if I'm going to have to have a real conversation with him to clear some stuff up. Which would suck because I've worked too damn hard to forget about that mess.

I'm almost never up until afternoon on the weekends, but since I've been sober, I can't seem to sleep in anymore. So I get up, send Brent a *leave me the fuck alone* text, then shower and smoke two cigarettes out my window before going downstairs to see what Mom's doing.

Dad is at the gym, sparring. I used to go with him. It was our bonding thing. It's how I got into boxing in the first place. At first he was impressed and thought it was cute to have an eleven-year-old who was such a good fighter. But then I got really good and it became a problem. Because young ladies from rich families don't box. That's for hood rats. I haven't touched my gloves since before I got my DUI, before I started drinking every day. It was a stupid idea in the first place. Not something I could ever really have.

When I got out of rehab my parents tried to do this family-meal-togetherness thing because they thought I'd fallen in with the wrong element due to lack of family bonding. But that lasted two days before Dad said he had too much work and I was fine anyway, just needed to realize my potential and stop spending time with wastes of space. Wonder what he would think of Joe and the *KILL* knuckles.

Mom blinks in surprise when she sees me now, her eyes red and her face splotchy.

"You've been crying?" I ask.

She takes a napkin and dabs off her face. "I'm fine. Just listening to some of those 'Stories of the Season.'"

I roll my eyes. Seriously. The radio station does these sad-sack stories twice a day where people call in and give all the details of their lame lives and then the radio station pays their heating bill or some shit. It's the stupidest fucking thing ever. Some woman talking about how she has incurable cancer and the radio deejay being all, "Well, you're in luck, because we're going to take care of your heating bill with the help of our very generous sponsor, Commonwealth Citizen." It's the worst kind of opportunistic douchery. And it ends with the cancer woman crying grateful tears as if she's super happy that she'll now be able to die in the comfort of a fully heated home.

"What was this one about?" I ask, grabbing a coffee mug from the cabinet and pouring myself a cup, adding a splash of peppermint creamer at the last second.

Mom dabs her face again. "It was about a woman whose daughter is addicted to meth. The daughter's been living on the streets and the mother wants to get her home for the holidays."

I raise an eyebrow. "The radio station is paying for rehab? Huh. That's pretty progressive."

Mom waves her hand. "No. Of course not. Nothing like that. But they're buying her all new clothes and paying for the mother's grocery bill so she can make a real family dinner for Christmas."

I snort. "So wait, the meth addict is getting a new wardrobe to show off to her pals on the street, and her mom is getting a ham and some green bean casserole? That radio station is so classy with the gift giving."

Mom's mouth pinches. "Don't be sarcastic. I thought you'd be more understanding of someone suffering from addiction."

I shake my head. "People who do meth are idiots and deserve whatever they get. Everyone has seen those pictures of the holes in the brain, and the teeth . . . Jesus."

I did meth once. It was fucking awesome. But disgusting junkie teeth are so not worth it. Plus the people you have to deal with to even score any are complete paranoid freaks.

"What are you doing today?" Mom asks. I knew meth talk would bring about a subject change. Shit was getting too real and Mom is a gold-star deflector. She's done it for years. It's why she's still with my dad.

"I thought I'd buy a pint and fill the ice cube trays with Jell-O shots."

Mom's eyes go wide.

"I'm just kidding." Though, actually, a smoothie with Bacardi in it would be outstanding about now.

"Natalie." It'd be better if it was a reprimand, but it's a plea. And I feel like an asshole.

"I don't know what I'm doing. I got homework to catch up on. I gotta find some friends who aren't loadies. I gotta buy another carton of cigarettes. You know? The usual."

This honesty is a new thing for me. I've never been honest with my mom—I'm still not about a lot of things and it's not like she's all that honest with me—but I feel like I owe her something because I know she thinks she's failed at parenting. I mean, she doesn't work, she only has one kid, she has a husband who barely even eats here, and she spends most of her time doing fund-raising for the art museum. It's all very 1950s mom, and a daughter who goes to rehab really puts a kink in that image.

"More cigarettes? You're seventeen. You don't want to start this habit. Studies have shown—"

I press my hands over my ears and start humming really loud. "I'm not listening to this," I holler.

Her mouth pinches and I release my hands.

"Mom. You're going to need to give me a pass on the ciga-rettes right now. I get how you feel, but I'm doing the best I can here."

Her face is sadness and love and concern and I want to slam my eyes shut and start this conversation over. "You used to have friends who weren't loadies," she says. "Camille."

"I used to have a lot of things," I snap back because I don't want to talk about Camille and how I used to be, and the best way to do that is to push Mom.

She draws in a deep breath. "Are you . . . ?" But she doesn't finish. Of course she doesn't finish. It's there, between us, but we won't talk about it.

"Would you like me to take you to a meeting?" she says instead.

I take a gulp of coffee—Jesus, that's good—and shake my head. "I don't think I'm going to one today. I'm already meeting my sponsor tomorrow morning and then I'm going to work this pancake breakfast so I can knock out that community service."

Mom's eyes light up. "Oh? You found community service to do."

"Yeah. Maybe. I was going to do some gift wrapping for children's literacy or whatever, but one of the guys at AA told me the judge won't count that."

"I don't see why not. It's work for a good cause." Her fingers fiddle with the napkin, folding it into some sort of origami boat. Mom really needs to get off Pinterest and get a job.

"Apparently the judge doesn't realize that getting a million wrapping paper cuts and being forced to deal with crabby holiday assholes for no money is legit community service. They actually want me to work with the less fortunate."

Mom's mouth droops. "Where's the pancake breakfast?"

"At SFC. It's not just a meeting place for drunks. Community stuff happens there too. Which basically means I'm going to be serving pancakes to a bunch of alkies and homeless guys, but whatever."

This is the longest conversation I've had with Mom in a while. It's almost like the whole thing is too much for her to process.

"Well, do they need more help? Because maybe I could . . ."

I hold up a hand and stop her. "Mom. Sobriety, community service, AA meetings, these are not mother-daughter bonding activities. This isn't book club. I know you're a total joiner, but trust me when I tell you this is one party you don't want to be invited to."

She's got the kicked-puppy face. I've hurt her feelings now. I feel like an ass. But honestly. Who does this? It's like my mom is so bored she even wants to co-opt the shitty things in my life.

I get up from the table before I feel even worse, and head upstairs. I one hundred percent do not want to feel bad about this. And usually when I don't want to feel something, I have a really solid solution. Only now I don't. Because Mom got rid of all the booze in the house except for Dad's super-expensive scotch, which he keeps *locked* in the bottom of the credenza.

I smoke a cigarette and watch as Mom trudges to each of the neighbors' houses to deliver tins full of cookies. Her shoulders are slumped and her red-and-green striped hat is lilting to the side. Shit.

I duck into my closet to grab a sweater and go help her, bracing myself for the twenty minutes of chitchat she'll partake in at every fricking house. As I'm pulling down a thick wool Lily McNeal striped cardigan, my boxing gloves fall from the side of the shelf where I'd tucked them forever ago. My chest freezes. I move my fingers over the laces and smell the leather. Tears push against the backs of my eyelids but I blink a bunch of times to stop them. I won't. I can't.

My right hand shakes as I slide it into the glove, just for a second. My knuckles curl on instinct, my whole arm tightening to swing. It's fast and hard and right into the back wall. Right through the drywall. I slump on the floor and let out a sob before tearing the glove off my hand. No. No. No no no. This isn't mine anymore.

I bolt from the closet, snag my phone, and text Brent. *I need fortification. Vodka and cranberry. Do NOT skimp on the vodka.*

He's at my house twenty minutes later. I chug down half the booze-filled water bottle before we say more than two sentences to each other. Then I give him a handy because I sort of owe him for doing me a solid.

"If you give me a few minutes, we could have sex?" He's

leaned back on my bed, catching his breath while I mop up his spunk with my nightshirt. At least he's nice enough to ask.

"Nah. I don't have any condoms," I say, and drink the rest of the vodka-cran. Jesus, that's good.

"Well . . . I could pull out. Oh. Sorry, shit. Maybe we could do other stuff or . . ." He looks like he is going to start in on the talking thing again, so I stroke him a few more times until he gets that sex-stupid look.

I'm *not* thinking about this. Not thinking about my past with Brent, and luckily, I've had enough vodka-cran to shut down my brain. "Mom's going to be done with cookie deliveries any minute. You better go."

He looks up at me. "You're serious?"

I nod. "Zip up, B. I'll catch you at school."

His dark eyes blink at me in shock. I don't know why he's so surprised. We're hardly the hang-around-and-chat-after-sex types. He pulls himself together and shakes his head, opening and closing his mouth a bunch of times like he wants to lay into me but can't find the words. Whatever. He's the only one who's come, so I'm not sure what he's got to complain about.

Resigned, he drops a kiss on my head, tucking my curly hair behind both my ears, and says, "I get that you're avoiding this, but we really do need to talk at some point."

I shake my head. "B. Stop aiming so high. We're not going to be a thing. Move on." I kiss him though, because I'm buzzing enough that I want to. "Thanks for the vodka."

He leaves and I collapse on my bed, staring at the ceiling as the buzz courses through me. It's not full-on drunk. I could've had at least two more water bottles, even though the vodka made up more than half the concoction. Still. It's been enough time that it feels good and it's better than Tylenol with codeine.

I end up texting Brent again an hour later when I see the hole in the wall of my closet.

Sorry. Come back?

What for?

Truth?

Please.

More fortification. Bring condoms.

His pause is way long and I think he's going to bail, despite my added incentive, but finally he answers, *Fine.*

When he gets to my room—past my mom, who doesn't offer anything but a polite "It's nice to see you, Brent" in her worried voice—I drop to my knees as soon as he shuts the door.

"Nat," he says, but then he shuts up real quick as I unbutton his pants.

I'm still buzzed enough that it's not a big deal, pulling out his dick and shoving down his boxers so they're cutting across the tops of his thighs. I'm also sober enough and motivated enough for more vodka not to be sloppy and make Brent realize I'm not that into this.

I used to hate the whole business of blowjobs, worrying if

it'd be rude to spit or pull off before he got too close to coming. Then one time when I was too wasted to do more than just let Brent shove himself in and out of my mouth, he came and it turned out swallowing it all really fast like a shot of shitty Jäger was much easier than stressing about spitting or dealing with him wanting to go longer.

"Nat," he says again as I work my tongue around him in circles. I hold his hip with one hand so he doesn't start trying to control the situation, and grip the base of him with the other hand so I barely have to do more than pay attention to the top inch of his junk.

"Enough," he says after a minute of my half-assed licking. "You're not even into it."

Shit. "I am," I lie.

"Give me a break," he says, pulling me onto my feet. "Talk."

"No." I try to drop down again, but he holds my elbows and looks at me hard.

"Nat."

"Where's my vodka-cran?"

He sighs and pulls two bottles from the inside of his Mark Jacobs down coat. I snag them and shimmy out of my jeans as I down the first bottle. I turn and am ready to pound the second bottle before we really get to things, but he's standing at my door, rebuttoning his pants. He has the saddest look on his face. Too many questions, too many answers, too many things we're supposed to say but I don't fucking want to.

"You're a dick," I say, my voice cracking.

"Yeah. So you say."

"Thought you said you wanted to have sex?" I wiggle, trying to distract him. Trying to do something to wipe the look off his face.

He shakes his head and opens the door. "Let me know when you're ready to talk."

He slips out of my room and it's the worst kind of sucker punch. I throw the empty bottle at the door and quickly uncap the second one, slamming it down even faster. This night needs to fade away.

Chapter
Ten

I wear my Prada sunglasses to my sponsor meeting with Kathy. She's already got a full cup of coffee and a half-eaten scone beside her when I get there. Plus the *Big Book* right in the middle of the table. I quickly glance around to see if anyone I recognize is here, since apparently my sponsor is as subtle as a car crash. No one is and I ease into the chair opposite her.

I point to the book. "Isn't there a pocket-sized version of that so we don't have to be so obvious?"

She rifles through her big pleather bag. Same one she had at the meeting. I almost feel guilty about the number of Coach and Kate Spade purses in my closet, but whatever, I can't help my parents being rich.

"As a matter of fact, there is." She hands me a mini *Big Book* and I drop it in my lap. "Are you ashamed of someone seeing you?"

"Yes. Duh. I mean, my friends know I went to rehab, but the

whole town doesn't. And my dad sort of wants to keep it on the down low."

Her face pinches. "Huh." She grabs the book and shoves it into her bag—yes, the bag is *that* big—and pulls out another mini. Which, okay, so she was testing me? And apparently carries an entire library in her bag.

"Lose the glasses," she says. I push them off my face and up to hold my hair back. My hair is loose and crazy, untamed curls because I woke up too late to shower.

"Yes, ma'am," I mumble.

She tips her head to the side. "You're hungover? Jesus."

"What? No, I'm not."

"Of course you are. I've seen that look in my own mirror more than once. It's not a bad hangover, but it's still a hangover."

She's right, but I don't say anything. Silence normally makes people think they're wrong or being judgmental. Unfortunately not with Kathy.

"That's strike one. Two more and I'm dropping you as a spons. I don't need the hassle, and if you're just playing, I'd prefer to have my Sunday mornings to myself, thank you very much."

"Why are you even doing this?"

She takes a sip of coffee and shrugs. "*My* sponsor told me it was time I get a spons of my own. It's the Twelfth Step, helping bring the message to others, practicing it in all aspects of our lives."

I smirk. "So? You need me as much as I need you."

"Hardly. There are always people looking for sponsors. Way more demand than supply at SFC. You're lucky I agreed to take you on."

I probably am, but I'm not about to admit it. Especially with my head pounding as much as it is. "So you said there were rules?"

She nods and pushes the plate of scone toward me. I shake my head because, gross, I'm not eating half of someone else's food, and also, I need grease right now.

"You need to call me every day you're not going to a meeting. I need you to meet me here once a week. I need you to call me if you're thinking of drinking again. I need you to shut up and listen."

"That all?"

"Yeah. It's not that hard."

She's basically just mandated that we're to be best girlfriends for an undetermined length of time. Sure, not that hard.

"I'm already at the Eleventh Step," I say.

She laughs. Not even shy. More like a horse laugh. The barista looks over at us and I slump a little in my chair. "You're not at the Eleventh Step. You don't even believe in God. I saw you mouthing 'watermelon' during the Lord's Prayer on Friday night."

Oh. Well, seriously. I'm sure half those women in there do the same thing. At least I'm not being hypocritical.

"Your first assignment is to read the chapter for the agnostics in the *Big Book*. It's called 'We Agnostics.'"

"I have a crap ton of homework to make up, Kathy. And I'm starting my community service today."

"Yeah. Joe told me about that. It'll be good for you. Meet some of the other guys at SFC. Get to know people in the program. But still. Read the chapter. Before next Sunday. It's not that long."

I've read it before. In rehab. My therapist suggested it when I first started arguing that God didn't exist. But if I'm being completely honest, I don't really remember much of it. Pretty much the only two things I remember about rehab were the itching need to either get drunk or get out. Most of the time both those things at once.

"Fine."

"You still have my number?" she asks, and I nod. "Good. Call me before school every morning you're not going to a meeting. What time is your first class?"

"Eight."

"Okay. I'm up by six. So call anytime after that. What days are you going to meetings?"

I shrug. "Haven't really locked in my schedule yet."

"Monday, Wednesday, Friday. Sundays with me, then pancake breakfast."

"Are you handling me?"

She shakes her head. "Not my job. I'm just trying to make

it as easy as possible for you to stay sober. Let's go outside and smoke."

Yes. Okay. This is good. This, I can deal with. Only as soon as we go outside and light up, she starts asking a bunch of personal questions about my family, my life, my DUI. And I'm wondering if this whole sponsor idea is not such a good one after all.

"Look, Natalie. I don't give a shit if you've got an attitude. Life can be crap sometimes and it's best you know that early. Then you won't be surprised when things go to hell. If you recognize nothing's perfect, you won't drink to make it go away, because you realize it never goes away. There's constant suffering. It's good you understand that."

"So today's lesson is: get used to suckiness? Bang-up job on the sponsoring, Kath. You're reeling me right into the program."

She snorts. "I'm not telling you anything you don't already know."

I blow a ring of smoke. "So how about you do that? Tell me something different. Give me some wisdom here, so peeling my eyes open this morning feels worth it."

"How about this one: everyone alcoholic, including you, princess, is a liar."

"I'm not . . . ," I start, but she waves her cigarette around.

"You are. And your attitude comes from the fact that you think everyone else is lying too. Not just the alcoholics. Everyone. And the reason you think that is because you lie all the time. That's what alcoholics do. And once you get real with the fact that more than likely you're the only liar in the room, you'll save yourself a ton of grief. And you'll start to trust people."

I want to snark back. I want to call her out on drinking the AA Kool-Aid without thinking critically about what a huge crock it all is, trusting some higher power to get yourself clean. Like some invisible dude in the sky is going to be able to make you say no when your friend is standing in front of you with a pitcher of margaritas or is going to swoop in when everything gets snatched away from you.

But I say nothing and take another drag of my cigarette. Kathy smiles.

"Good. You're already learning. Shut up and listen. You'll get out of the hole eventually."

Chapter
Eleven

The pancake breakfast is hopping. Which means a bunch of super-old guys who reek of cigarettes and pee are waiting in a line for someone to hand them a Styrofoam plate containing two sausages and three pancakes drowned in syrup. Joe's standing behind the tub of sausages, tonging two onto a plate, then passing the plate to a younger woman who adds pancakes and a soup ladle of syrup. She offers a big smile to every one of the dudes she passes a plate to.

Kathy joins the back of the line and points me to Joe.

"Unless you want to eat first?" she adds.

"Um, no. Gross." I'm about to ask her if maybe our little coffee chat this morning counted as a reason to sign my court card, but I don't want to push it after she called me out for being hungover.

I walk over to Joe with my head up and my shoulders back. I splashed some water on my face at Starbucks so I'm feeling much better. He sees me and shakes his head.

"You're going to need a hairnet for that hair. And if you show up again hungover, I'm sending you home."

Jesus. Do these people have some sort of built-in sobriety chip?

"You're not the boss of me." Okay, I'm five. But whatever. A hello would've been nice.

"No. She is. Natalie, this is Kara. Kara, this is Natalie. Nat's got community service hours. She can help you out for probably the next five or six months."

Kara beams at the same time I sputter, "Six months?"

He looks at me, gaze darting over my face, then down the rest of me in a quick perusal. "How many hours do you have?"

"A hundred."

He lifts a shoulder. "Well, there you go. Five hours once a week. Twenty weeks. You'll be here the next five months, give or take, depending on holidays and your schedule. I thought you were good at math?"

"Fuck off."

He laughs. Kara is still smiling wide and handing plates to the guys in line. She's put so much syrup on each plate the sausages look as if they're floating in a moat.

"You probably could ease up on the syrup," I suggest.

"Oh. You know syrup? Great. You can do that. I'll hand the plates to you, you add the syrup, and give them to the guys. Our regular syrup guy is in Florida."

"Lucky," I mumble before sliding next to her. Joe chuckles and pulls something from a box behind him before handing it to me.

I look at it. "Hairnet? You were for real about that?"

"Of course I was. No one wants to come across one of those curls while they're eating. Put it on."

"Yes, sir." I stick out my tongue and he laughs at me again.

"I know you're meeting with Kathy on Sunday mornings, but you'll need to do that earlier. We need you here by eight for setup. Breakfast is nine to noon. An hour of cleanup afterward."

"I'm supposed to meet Kathy earlier than eight? Are you fucking kidding me?"

"No," he says, and it's clear he's not. "She's good for it. She's usually up by six. You can meet her at seven."

"A.m.?"

"Jesus, Natalie, a lot of people are up at seven in the morning."

I know. My dad is one of them. A long time ago I was one too. But that was when I boxed and had training and thought I might be something other than what I am. Now, even the idea of a Sunday-morning chitchat with my dad before I have to go freeze my ass off at the crack of dawn to meet with my sponsor makes me want to spew venom.

"Maybe I'll figure out a different time to meet her," I mumble.

"That's between you two. But we need you here by eight. Now put on the hairnet."

I tug my hair back into a half-baked braid and slide the hairnet over it. I don't even want to think about what I must look like. I slip back beside Kara, who's been completely ignoring us. I look at her wide smile and wonder if maybe she's a little dim.

She shows me the vat of syrup and hands me the ladle. "I love syrup so much, but some of the guys say that I sometimes overdo it."

I bite back a retort and instead offer my own smile. "I'll do my best."

Two hours in and we've had a steady stream of people the entire time. I've gone through two packs of gum and had three cigarette breaks, and luckily, Joe or Kara hasn't said a thing about it. Calvin comes from the back and replaces all of our food just when it's getting low, as if he has a Spidey sense about it.

He blinks in surprise when he sees me.

"Community service," I mumble.

He grins and I see he's missing one of his top teeth. "Joe's taken on another pet project? That guy never learns." He chuckles to himself and I feel my face flush.

I want to argue I'm no one's project, but I'm speechless over the idea that I'm not Joe's first effort at helping someone. And now I wonder about him and Kathy and what the real story there is. And worse, I'm sort of really feeling the vodka from last night.

I grow increasingly sullen as I put half a ladle of syrup on every plate. The people in front of me are friendly, but probably more because they get to taste their food without so much syrup. They ask how I'm doing and I mumble "fine" more times than I can count.

I don't even realize it's noon until Joe nudges me. "What's wrong with you?"

"What? What do you mean?"

"Where's the snarky girl who has something to say about everything?"

"Was Kathy a pet project?" I blurt out.

He runs his hand through his dark blond hair, and I wonder if it's soft or smells like dude shampoo. "Kathy's my ex-sister-in-law. She was married to my brother until she fucked it up by becoming a drunk. When he finally left her, he gave her my number and told her I could help."

"How long has she been sober?" I ask.

"About two years, I think. Maybe a little more."

I nod. "So I'm your pet project?"

I don't know why I care about this. I don't know why it would matter. He's older than me. By a lot. So's Kathy. None of these people can be real friends to me. I'm not even sure what I want from any of them.

"Grab the syrup. We need to take these back to the kitchen to clean."

I nod and follow him to the kitchen. Calvin's there with two of his buddies. Sous-chefs, I guess. One of them is the Hispanic guy who slept through my first meeting. He looks sober and lucid right now. And young. Younger than I thought.

"You look like shit, *querida*. You allergic to work or hung-over?" he says.

"Both," I answer, and his face breaks into a huge grin.

"I'm Alex." He holds his hand out and I shake it. He's tall. Like over six feet. And his skin is a beautiful brown. "You working the program?"

I nod. "And doing community service."

"Open bottle in your car?" he asks.

I blush. "DUI."

It's gotten really quiet, so I turn around. Joe's staring at the two of us, gaze darting back and forth between our faces. "No," he says. "Alex hasn't even gotten a full month yet. Not a good idea for either of you."

I laugh hard. Apparently the mating rituals in AA involve a heavy dose of honesty. "Take it easy. We haven't even exchanged numbers. I don't think you need to book the banquet hall."

Joe shakes his head. "Alex is a player. He sleeps with all the young girls. Ask him."

Alex mutters something in Spanish.

I turn back to Alex and ask, "You clean?"

"Today I am," he says with a smile. "You want me to do a Breathalyzer?"

"No. I mean clean of STDs."

He smiles. "Oh, I like you. Yes, I'm always safe. Not into being a baby daddy."

Without thinking too much, I pull out my phone. "Okay then. Give me your number."

Joe steps in and snatches the phone from my hand. "Can I talk to you outside?" he snarls.

I wink at Alex, then follow Joe out the door into the hallway.

"What the hell are you doing? Didn't you hear anything I just said?"

"Yeah, Dad. Thanks for your concern. But I'm not terribly worried about getting my heart broken by an alkie. I just like to have backup in case I need an itch scratched."

His eyebrows draw up. "Backup? Do you already have a boyfriend?"

Which, huh. He looks uncomfortable and I'm not even sure what to make of that. "Nope. No boyfriend. You interested?"

He shakes his head and looks at the floor. "You're a kid. And you're playing games. You need to pull your shit together and get with the program. You're not at a frat house. You're not here to date. You're here to get sober. Period."

I step into his space and he goes very still. There's a thing here; he must feel it as much as I do. But I'm not stupid enough to get involved with this sort of accident waiting to happen. Usually.

It is fun to mess with him, though.

I reach my hand out and squeeze his before he can shake

it off. "Are you offering me an alternative to Alex? Will you scratch my itch?"

He lets out a long breath. "No. I'm too old and you need a friend more than anything else. But I'll tell you this: Alex is a liar. The last girl who came through here left with a case of herpes. It's your life, but herpes are impossible to get rid of."

He steps away from me, hands me my phone, and heads back into the kitchen. I stare at my reflection in the glass on one of the pictures hanging in the hallway. I'm still wearing my hairnet. I rip it off and follow Joe into the kitchen, avoiding Alex enough that finally he gets up, flips Joe off, and leaves through the back entrance.

Chapter
Twelve

Joe's not at the Monday-afternoon meeting, but Alex is. I sit on the opposite side of the room to him and keep my head down most of the hour. The STD thing is enough to discount him as a possibility, but it feels a little good to peek up at him and see he can't keep his eyes off me. I pull the "I'd just like to listen" card and then spend the rest of the meeting counting the minutes on the clock.

Twenty seconds after the Lord's Prayer, I bolt to my car and light a cigarette. I swipe my hand across my phone and consider calling Brent. He's probably somewhere partying. Amy and Amanda are also an option, but I don't feel up to dealing with them drunk. They're the kind of girls who think everything is hilarious when they're drinking. And I don't think they could help me shake whatever it is that grips me when I walk out of a meeting. I see Alex heading to his truck and consider him for a second—if we used a condom and were really careful—but herpes is the gift that keeps on giving and I need a quick fix, not a long-term problem.

In the end I stub out my cigarette and head home. When I walk in the front door, I see an elf has been shoved in between two spindles on the stairs.

"Mom," I call. "There's an elf out here with his head stuck in the banister."

"Oh," she says in this chipper voice. "You already found Elfie?"

She walks into the room and I patently ignore the HO HO HO sweater she's wearing.

"Who's Elfie?"

She goes over to the elf and slides his head out before holding him up. "Elfie. He's our Elf on the Shelf. You're supposed to find him every day."

My eyes go wide. "You're serious?"

She beams. "Yes. If you find him every day, it means you'll have a *very* good Christmas this year."

I let out a long sigh. "Is this another sobriety test? If I can't find the elf, are you going to be worried I've hit the bottle again?"

She bristles. "Don't be ridiculous. There's a Breathalyzer on your car and you're going to meetings and seeing Dr. Warner."

I drop down onto the top stair and Mom squeezes in beside me, her hands flitting over the elf's plastic clothes.

"Mom, you're going to need to start trusting me again,

not just counting on pee tests and Breathalyzers."

Her hands stop moving and she draws in a long breath. "It had been going on a while, Natalie. The DUI wasn't the first time. Do you think I didn't know?"

So. We're actually going to have this conversation. "You drink. Dad drinks."

She shakes her head. "In moderation. And we're not seventeen. Your dad thinks . . ."

She bites her lip and I stare at her. "Go ahead. Tell me what he thinks . . ."

"He thinks it's just a phase. A teenager thing. But, Natalie, my father . . . well, it's just not something you want to get too attached to."

I almost laugh. "Your dad was an abusive alkie who drank his way through his liver before he was fifty-five. Nana told me. I'm not too worried about following in those footsteps."

She reaches a hand for mine and I don't shake her off like I usually do. "He was. But, Natalie, you've always been this kind of person."

I drop her hand. "What kind of person?"

"The kind of person who doesn't know how to say stop. Who doesn't know when enough is enough. Look at how you were when you were boxing. Always at the ring, always training. You'd come home with bruises and be limping and still you'd be back there the next day."

I shrug. "Until Dad stopped taking me."

"We just thought it would be better if you eased back a little. You were so intense about it."

"I haven't been in the ring in forever."

She shakes her head. "Yeah. You quit boxing and you started drinking. It's always something with you. That's your personality. When you were a little girl, if I let you pour your own cereal you'd eat the whole box. If I didn't monitor your TV watching, you'd finish a whole series in one night. You were even like that with your friends. You'd spend all your time with someone and then it was like you were done. You're all or nothing and it's not a good way to be. Because you'll never learn balance."

I stand up and the tension is so bad in my neck that I have to roll my shoulders a few times. "I don't know how to say stop? I don't know when enough is enough? This, coming from the woman who has been married to a cold prick incapable of loving anyone but himself. That's rich. Maybe you need to worry a little bit less about me, and creating the perfect holiday season, and worry a little more about the state of your life."

I snatch the elf from the stair. "And I'm not playing 'find the elf' every day. Meetings, community service, Dr. Warner. That's my life. I'm filling my card up, and the minute graduation's over, I'm out of here."

"Natalie. Calm down. Stay and talk to me. We haven't—"

"No. Fuck off, Mom. You don't really want to talk. You want me to say the things you want to hear. I'll be home later."

I grab my keys and my purse and pretend I don't hear the sob that escapes her mouth as I slam the door. My hands are shaking so much I can barely hold the Breathalyzer to my mouth and start the car. Once I get going, I light a cigarette and go through two more before I realize where I'm headed.

The gym is exactly the same. I walk in and inhale deeply and it's like coming home to a plate of Christmas cookies, the peanut butter ones with the Hershey's kisses on top. The disgusting body odor is like a magic aroma. Walls a shitty gray-white, mostly covered with fight posters and photos of former boxers. A set of tires on the floor right next to the entrance for practicing footwork. There are a few guys sparring in the ring and a couple of others on the weight benches or jumping rope. A girl is in the corner, pounding on one of the bags her trainer is holding. He looks up and smiles when he sees me before saying something to the girl and heading my way.

"Natalie. I never thought you'd darken our doors again," he says as he approaches.

"Just seeing if the place was still standing. It's good to see you, Josh."

He grins. "You too, girl. You here to suit up?"

"Nah. I'm in no shape for it."

"Gotta start somewhere."

I'm tempted. So tempted that I almost drop my coat where I'm standing, but then a voice sounds from behind me.

"This isn't a drop-in gym. Natalie made her decision a long time ago. Unless she's changed her mind, she needs to run along and you need to get back to work."

Josh looks past my shoulder and I turn to see Jerry. No smile of greeting, just the same cold eyes and hard face he's always had.

"Jerry. It's good to see you too," I say.

He comes up and for a second I think he might hug me, but instead he throws a punch that stops less than two inches from my face. I flinch.

"Your reflexes are slow. You drunk?"

I shake my head. "In and out of rehab, actually. Working the twelve-step program. All clean and sober."

His dark skin and bald head make him look tough on the outside, but that pales in comparison to how he is on the inside. Unflappable. Nothing bothers him. His mother could die and he'd be back at work the same day. For a long time I thought he didn't have any emotions. But the day I showed up drunk after months of being MIA, I knew he did. I'd never seen him so pissed.

"So you coming back to train for real?"

I look at my feet and shake my head. When I glance up I see Jerry wave Josh away. Josh nods at me and squeezes my shoulder. "Good to see you, Nat."

I nod back but can't push words past the lump in my throat.

"Do you want to talk to me?" Jerry asks.

"No," I whisper.

"Then what are you doing here?"

"I don't know." It was a bad idea. This isn't an option. It's not in the cards for me. But God, I miss it so much.

"Still not ready then. Suit yourself. Don't come back again unless you mean it. I don't like surprise visitors."

For a second I think I see disappointment on his face, but then his expression drops back into his hard mask. I nod my head and move toward the door. My feet feel like they have cement blocks strapped to them. I never should have come.

My hands are shaking as I start my car. I squeeze my eyes shut and then slam on the accelerator and speed out of the gym parking lot. I'm going way too fast for the ice on the road, but I can't slow down. I'm dizzy with the need to fight, but there's nothing I can do. I light a cigarette and inhale three times before I have enough sense to pull over.

I call Joe without thinking too hard about it.

"Where are you?"

"Natalie. Good to hear from you. I'm at a job site. Everything okay?"

His voice is strangely soothing and allows me to take a deep breath. "Yes. No. I don't know. I guess. I had a fight with my mom." I almost tell him about the gym, but I'm not sure how much I want Joe poking around in my past.

"Do you want to meet me here? I'm almost done with the job. We could get coffee."

"Yeah. Okay. Will I be bothering you? I don't want to get you fired."

He laughs. "It's fine. I'm my own boss. I won't get fired. Do you know the empty lot on Madison where the gas station used to be?"

"Yeah."

"That's where I am. I'll wait for you."

I'm about to click off, but at the last second I remember to say "Thanks."

"Yep."

Fifteen minutes later I'm out of cigarettes and standing on the edge of a large empty lot, leaning against Joe's pickup truck.

"What exactly do you do?" I vaguely remember his business card, but this seems like a good conversation starter.

He smiles and a little more of the tension eases out of me. "Well, the people who bought this lot are going to build a child-care center on it. And they're interested in making it as eco-friendly as possible: using recycled materials, collecting rainwater to use later for watering the garden, heating it using the earth's resources."

I have no idea what any of this has to do with Joe, but I just want him to keep talking so I can forget the gym, Jerry's words, and my mom telling me I don't know how to say stop.

"Anyway, I'm a geothermal specialist. I work on developing heating and cooling systems using the earth's core to regulate temperature. So I mostly work with contractors and architects."

"You're an eco guy? Really?"

He laughs. "Yeah. Really."

"Huh." There's a pause and I try to put this new information into the file I'm making in my head on Joe, but it doesn't quite fit. "Well, Joe, to be honest, that's sort of unexpected. I mean, not to be a dick, but were you doing this before you were drinking? Because this seems pretty ambitious and a little hard to pull off if you're stumbling around trying to shake off a bender."

"Yeah. That's true. But I've met drunks who were doctors and lawyers and all sorts of ambitious professions and somehow they faked it for a lot of years. Though in my case, I learned about all this stuff after. First with some books I found in the prison library, and then afterward I went to school for it."

I want to step into his space again, but I don't have the energy to mess with him. I need someone to talk to and in this moment he's the best I've got. "So."

"So?" He waits and I don't know what to say now. Not that I'm tongue-tied so much as I'm tired and it feels like too much. He must see it because he says, "Let's go to the oasis and get some coffee. We'll come back for your car later."

He opens his passenger door and helps me in. Nothing

flirty, just a sturdy hand on my arm. He slips into the driver's side and pops open the glove compartment to a pack of Parliaments.

I take one and inhale deeply, looking out the side window at the gross Chicago winter gray. There's silence for a long while and I consider asking him to turn on the radio, but instead I say, "My mom says I don't know how to say stop."

"Is she right?"

I shrug. "I haven't really thought about it. I mean, why stop? Drinking's fun. It's relatively harmless. A lot of people do it."

He nods and maneuvers his truck into the oasis. "Does it seem the same when you do it as when they do it?"

I turn toward him. "What do you mean?"

He opens his door and then comes around to my side to let me out. Like we're on a date. Which, weird. "For me, I always thought we all drank, so it wasn't a big deal. It was social. I was the life of the party. It was nothing. But then I noticed I'd be starting earlier than everyone else. Drinking longer. Way past the time when they'd quit so they could sober up to get home. And I saw how I was the only one who drank every day. I'd have friends who gave it up for Lent or for the month of February, or for a few months while they were training for a bike race, or whatever. But me, I couldn't imagine giving up for that long. I mean, I'd wake up and think, I'm gonna dry out today, but by noon, I'd be at it again. And once I had one, I was off. No stopping mechanism on me."

A chill runs through me and Joe pulls off his wool cap and drops it on my head, pulling it tightly over my ears.

"You need to wear hats. You got a lot of hair, but that's not going to protect you in the winter."

"Thanks, Dad."

"Cut that out."

He holds the door to the oasis open and I lead him in. "What?"

"Stop calling me Dad. I feel old enough around you."

I smirk. "Should I go with Pops instead?"

"You're hilarious. How do you like your coffee?"

"With a lot of sugar and a lot of milk."

He rolls his eyes. "Of course."

When he gets back to the table, I've warmed up enough to return his hat and peel off my coat. He takes his coat off too and sits across from me.

"Was your DUI the first time you tried to get sober?"

He shakes his head. "No. But it was the first time I got serious about it. I sort of had no choice, being in prison. Terrible case of DTs for my first five days there. And the Illinois Department of Corrections isn't very forgiving of drunks. I had to suffer on my own. Didn't get out of bed, didn't eat, just had to wait them out. It was almost enough for me to never drink again. But of course, I backslid a bunch of times after I got out."

I take a gulp of coffee and smile at how light and sweet it is. Perfect. Almost like hot chocolate. "What finally got you to give it up for good?"

He shakes his head. "It's a long story for another time. First I want to know how much you want it."

"How much I want what?"

"To be sober."

His stare is hard to look away from. And I know I'm going to have to be honest for both our sakes. "I don't really know. I don't want to be addicted to alcohol, but your story, Kathy's story, Alex's story, whatever, that's not me. My DUI wasn't a call for help, or me hitting rock bottom. I was stupid and drunk, driving someone home who was more stupid and drunk."

"So." He folds his hands in front of him. "I guess that puts you closer to Step One: admit you're powerless over alcohol and that your life has become unmanageable."

I shrug.

"Are you even there yet?"

I close my eyes and remember the conversation with my mom. Remember what it was like when I boxed, how I didn't think I could ever re-create that high after I walked away from it. And how drinking got me pretty close to it. Then I think about the handy and the half-assed blowjob I gave Brent. The accident and the DUI. The orange juice and vodka I had in my water bottle almost every day of the past year.

The Tylenol with codeine. The Breathalyzer on my car.

"Yeah," I say finally. "I guess I'd say things are a bit unmanageable."

He nods. No judgment, just Joe's solid impassive face. "Well, then, welcome to AA."

Chapter
Thirteen

I'm nine days sober now and nine days since any of my friends at school have said one word to me. I've bumped into Camille a couple of times again, but she hasn't asked any more questions, just searched my face—probably checking to see if I'm sober—and walked on with her honors-track friends. Brent stares at me all the fricking time, but when I finally asked, "What the hell are you looking at?" he turned and walked away without saying anything.

He's waiting. I get that. Everyone's waiting. Part of me is sort of waiting too, if I'm honest. Waiting to figure out what is going to get me to drink again. Because every day I stand at my locker and count to ten and think: I should find Amy and Amanda and get a water bottle filled up with peppermint schnapps. That's festive.

Mostly the only thing that keeps me from doing it is Kathy's daily phone calls of cantankerous advice and Joe's texts. And

Mom's goddamn Elf on the Shelf, which she now has hidden in the most ridiculous places imaginable: tampon box, in my bra drawer, in the cookie tin I keep eating from, in the jar of gum packs I constantly chew, in my carton of cigarettes. He's like the Jiminy Cricket of the Twelve Steps. And damn if I'm not sober partly because of his stupid plastic face.

I reread the chapter about agnostics in the *Big Book*. Kathy even let me fight with her about God and didn't care that I thought a lot of people were putting their eggs in a basket that had a giant hole in the bottom of it. She only shrugged and said, "It's an awfully big world for you to assume everything in it has to do with you." Which, whatever, okay.

I've worked another pancake breakfast, and Joe and I amused the people going through the line with our arguments over every stupid thing: sausages or bacon, Cubs or Sox, chocolate or vanilla, red or black licorice. By the end I realized he was disagreeing just for the sake of pissing me off—no one chooses black licorice over red—which made me want to fling syrup at him. But the five hours went by really fast.

On sober day ten I'm walking out of school when I see Brent, Amy, and Amanda waiting at the bike racks. My feet slow as I approach them.

"How's it going, Nattie?" Amy says. Her hair is up and she's not wearing a hat and I can't believe she's not freezing because it feels to me like my fingers are about to fall off.

"Good. What's up?"

Amanda stands and sways a bit, which answers the question as to why they don't seem to be cold. "My parents are out for two days. I'm at home with my brother, but he's already disappeared. Wanna come over?"

Amanda's brother is fifteen and doesn't ever talk to us. He plays video games in his room and treats everyone like crap. Amanda says he's been like that since his girlfriend cheated on him. I suspect he's been like that since birth.

"I gotta go to a meeting."

Amy snort-sighs. "Come on. Skip it. We'll fake a signature on your court card. They don't really check those anyway."

Which is probably a good point and I'm surprised I haven't thought of this myself. But still, as much as I could use a drink, boozing with the A's is not appealing.

"I'll pass. You guys need a ride, though?" Because really, they're still my friends and none of them look like they're in any shape to drive.

Brent steps up. "No. I got my car."

He's not swaying, but his eyes definitely aren't the most clear they've ever been. This is hardly my problem. Two months ago I wouldn't have given the first shit. Two months ago I would've driven, probably way more wasted than any of them are now. But frickin' Joe and his drive into the White Hen and my accident with the stop sign are too fresh in my mind.

"Give me your keys. I'll take you."

Brent holds his keys up and I reach for them, but he snatches them away. "You're not driving my Escalade. Come on, girls."

Amy and Amanda stumble after him, and I dig through my pockets for my keys. I'm going to have to follow them now. Jesus.

I'm heading toward my car when Mrs. Hunt calls out to me. I scan to see how far Brent and the girls have gotten, but they're still fumbling outside Brent's car, snorting and giggling.

"It's not a great time, Mrs. Hunt."

Her mouth pinches when she approaches. "I'm sorry I don't fit into your busy schedule. But we need to have a conversation about your incomplete assignments. I'd like to set some expectations about dates and how to get you caught up to the rest of the class."

Brent slides into the driver's seat and the A's tumble into the back. My gaze returns to Mrs. Hunt and I can see she's watching them too. And I can see every thought she's having, but I frankly don't care. She can think what she's going to think. I need to follow Brent.

"Yeah, Mrs. Hunt, we can have that conversation. Just not right now. I'll come to see you tomorrow after school, okay? I gotta go."

"I'm going to have to start giving you zeroes, Natalie. Don't you care if you graduate?"

I nod. "I do care. But there is other stuff going on right now and sometimes we just have to make the best choice we can at the moment. I'm sorry. I'll talk to you tomorrow."

I wave, then bolt from her and slam into my car, exhaling into the Breathalyzer so I can get the engine started. Brent and the girls are already down the block, but he's driving slow so it doesn't take much time to catch up to him. I don't even think he realizes I'm following them. At one of the stop signs, he pauses for way too long and I almost get out of the car to see what's going on. But then he jerks forward, weaving a tiny bit.

My phone rings. Joe.

"You're not at the meeting," he says by way of introduction.

"I'm following drunk friends home."

"What?"

I sigh. "Not like that. I'm following them home because they're drunk and they wouldn't let me drive them and I just want to make sure they get home okay."

"You should call the cops, Natalie."

"No way."

"What do you hope to accomplish by following them? Do you think you're going to stop an accident? How? By driving your car in the middle of it?"

Well, okay, good point. Maybe I didn't think this through. "I can't call the cops. They're my friends and I'm not a narc."

He huffs. "Friends. Yeah. You probably need to upgrade who you're spending time with."

"What? To ex-cons and STD carriers? Stop being so judgmental."

"Stop being so naive."

"Fuck off, Joe. I'm not dumping my friends because they didn't end up in rehab with me."

He laughs. It's sort of dark and bitter, and I hate that I'm having this conversation as I follow Brent home. "That's not why you dump your friends. You dump your friends because they're enablers. Because they keep you sick. But most of the time, you don't even need to dump them. They'll dump you as soon as they realize you won't party with them anymore. I've been there."

"Well, maybe I have a higher caliber of friend than you do. Maybe everything that happens to me isn't *exactly* how it happened to you. Maybe you haven't 'been there' when it comes to *my* friends."

I'm clenching the steering wheel so hard with my left hand I can feel my knuckles turning white beneath my winter gloves. Joe can be such a paternalistic dick. I don't even know why I'm listening to him.

"You know what? We're done. I don't need this crap—" I start.

"Natalie," he says, and it's a plea. Stark and honest and very Joe. "I'm sorry. You're right. Your friends might be different. I should only be telling you about my experience, not assuming you're having the same one. But Jesus, you're following drunk people home at three o'clock in the afternoon. You have to know that you deserve better friends than this."

I let out a long sigh. "Why? Why do I deserve better than

this? What do I have to offer anyone, really? You want me to put myself in my higher power's hands, but why would He want me? I'm a fucking mess. I deserve shit friends because I *am* a shit friend. I've been a shit friend for a long time. Why would anyone worth anything want to stick with me? If I'm not drinking and entertaining people, I've got nothing to offer anyone."

Sweet Jesus, I just said that out loud. It's like Kathy and her crusty badgering are getting to me and I'm blurting out things I never would have. Or maybe it's being frazzled by following the A's home. Either way, I want to swallow it back, rewind the last few minutes and not even talk to Joe at all.

"Is that what you think?" His voice is so soft I almost don't hear it. "You think people don't want anything to do with you because you have no value? You think God doesn't?"

It's a punch to the gut, because it's exactly what I think. What I've thought for a while. If there even is a God, why the hell would He want me on His side? I'm the reason He flooded the earth before Noah's ark. I'm the human equivalent of a need for a do-over. The one on the team who you can't wait to be subbed out so they don't ruin your chances for a win.

By now I've pulled over to the side of the road and I'm crying hard. Too many things are pressing against my brain and I have to fight hard to keep the worst of them locked away. Brent's car is parked in Amanda's driveway and they've all gone in. I'm not sure how much I've said to Joe, but I said enough out loud that he's hushing me and asking me where I am.

Finally I sniff and say, "I'm fine. I'm heading home. I'll talk to you tomorrow."

"Come to the meeting. I'll meet you there. We'll go in late. Just come."

I'm too tired and too wrung out, but I agree to go because if I don't, I won't be able to get Joe off the phone. He's that guy. That friend. And as I watch my other friends dance and spin in the living room of Amanda's house, drinking out of a bottle in front of her large bay window, I say a little prayer to a maybe-God to be worthy of a better friend. Because I'm pretty sure my old ones aren't going to work out.

Chapter
Fourteen

Christmas Eve brings an end to Elfie's hiding, with his final resting place being the base of the tree next to gobs of presents I'm sure none of us really need. It's incredibly quiet in the house this year, and I feel like both my parents are moping because they didn't have a party. I tell them a hundred times they could still invite the neighbors over, but Mom holds her ground and instead we have a somber meal on formal china.

Mom cajoles us both into going to church, which I'm actually okay about. I'm on the Third Step with Kathy and we've been talking a lot about things we have no control over and giving those things up to the universe. Church seems as good a place as any to let go of a bunch of crap I can't do a damn thing about. Which Kathy says is pretty much the same as putting my faith in a higher power.

Christmas Eve service at church is a pageant with a bunch

of overtired kids, who all signed up to be angels or animals, so there's only one magus and no shepherds. Mary and Joseph are usually played by the couple who had a baby most recently, so most of the service is hard to hear because of a screaming Baby Jesus. It's pretty hilarious and completely disorganized. Which is one of the things I always liked about our church. Before I stopped going because I was too hungover to knuckle through it.

Our church is really mission based, so they're always mixing everyone up, pushing diversity and integration and all of us being children of God. There's one big service: kids, old people, homeless guys, my parents. Together in one place. Tonight I catch sight of a couple of guys from AA who nod and smile at me. Dad glares at them when they give me a thumbs-up.

"Chill," I mumble. "They're from my meetings."

"Wonderful," he says. "Maybe you should invite them to the house afterward. That would cap off the evening pretty well."

"Don't be sarcastic in church, Tom," Mom says, which makes me snort.

At the end of the service, one of the girls from the high school youth choir sings "O Holy Night." I've seen her at school before, but she runs with a way cleaner crowd than me. Not that I'm running with any crowd right now. Her name is April, I think. Her voice sounds like an angel's and even Dad shuts up with the snarky comments after she sings.

On the way home I get a text from Joe.

Make it through the day?

I smile.

Yeah. You?

I should've asked him his plans. It occurs to me now that he might be alone and the thought of that makes me ache a little.

Kathy and I burned lasagna and went out for Chinese.

My stomach tightens and I pretend I don't feel jealous, but it's no use. And I'm at the point now where I can't lie to Joe about it.

I wish I could've been with you guys. Dinner was filet mignon served with a side of angry father and placating mother.

My phone pings back right away.

Sounds delicious. SFC is open all day tomorrow. 24 hours because there are lots of people who are orphans at Christmas and it's one of the hardest times to stay sober.

I look at Mom and Dad in the front seat. Not talking to each other. Neither smiling. Dad looking at stocks on his phone while he's driving as if the market is still open. Mom holding on to her seat belt as if she's anticipating imminent death.

You going?

Not sure. Are you booked all day?

Hardly. Belgian waffles in the morning, then presents, usually done by 11 a.m.

O'Hare Oasis is open too, if you want to have some biscuits before stop-
ping by SFC.

Noon?

It's a plan.

I can't stop the grin from spreading on my face. I should
feel bad that I'm bailing on Mom, but I honestly don't. Two
Christmases ago I went to the gym after opening presents
and sparred with Josh because I didn't want to deal with
Mom's *A Christmas Story* marathon. Then I came home to a
lecture from Dad and a mandate to stop boxing. Which I
ultimately complied with. Last Christmas I was loaded by
eleven a.m. from spiked eggnog and a few snorts of Ritalin.
All things considered, my attendance this year shouldn't be
required, really.

"I'm going to SFC tomorrow after we do presents," I say,
leaning forward a bit so I rest my hand on Mom's shoulder.

"What? No. Natalie. We're spending the day together as a
family."

I shake my head. "We did that today. We've had plenty of
quality time. And SFC is open all day because a lot of people
have a tough time on holidays."

I'm totally playing the pity card, but I don't want to make a
big deal of this.

Mom turns back to me. "Well, is it open for everyone?
Because maybe we could bring over some food and—"

I wave my hand. "No. Mom. No. It's only for the alkies."

This probably isn't true. And I'm pretty sure no one would turn my mom away at the door if she were holding a roasted ham and a bunch of her cookies, but I don't want her to be part of this. Part of me and Joe and our day.

Her head drops for a second and she lets out a little sigh. I feel like a huge asshole, but I just can't deal with them for another day.

"If that's what you want, Natalie. I'll drive you over."

"Nonsense, Sarah," Dad interjects. "That's why I fixed up her car. She can drive herself, and you and I can join Steven and his wife for their Christmas cocktail party. I'm sure I can call tonight and let him know we've had a change of plans."

Dad's so enthused about this I'm a little sick. I almost want to tell him to forget it just so he has to suffer with my company. But the carrot of Joe is too big to resist. "See, Mom? You and Dad have plans. It's going to be fine. I'll go to SFC, do a meeting, they'll probably have a speaker or something, then I'll come home. No big deal."

Mom's shoulders slump. "Okay."

Joe's already at Popeyes when I slide into the seat across from him on Christmas. A box in red candy-cane wrapping paper and a green bow is sitting on the table.

"Shit. We're exchanging gifts? I don't have anything for you. You didn't say."

He smiles. "It's not necessary. And I don't need anything.

But this, you need. Well, you actually don't need it. But . . . just open it."

I'm curious and I have no patience and I hate surprises, so I rip it open like a little kid and he laughs.

"Joe," I say with a big grin. "You bought me a carton of cigarettes. You are a Christmas miracle."

"This is the part where I tell you that you probably shouldn't smoke. You're young and it's a nasty habit."

"And yet here I sit with this spectacular gift and it's perfect. And saves you from having to give up half your supply."

He gives me a partial grin and my stomach whoops, and yeah, that needs to stop happening. I look at the cigarettes and swallow down all the things I could say but definitely should not.

"Oh wait," I say at last. "I do have a gift for you."

I dig through my bag and pull out a pen. "Close your eyes," I tell Joe. He closes them and I dig out Elfie. I write the letters *KILL* on his little plastic fingers, holding in my laughter as I do it. "Okay, you can open them."

Joe looks at Elfie and blinks. I hold up the plastic hand with *KILL* on it and he laughs. "It's perfect."

"Yeah. Elfie's just like you. Seemingly all chipper and put together, but he totally has a dark side."

"You think I have a dark side?"

I nod and take Joe's hand. Which maybe I shouldn't have done because I don't really want to give it back now. And I'm pushing, but I can't help myself. I trace the letters on his knuckles and he doesn't pull away and I look at his face, and I know he's right there with me.

"So. How'd you end up with this tattoo?"

He shakes his head and pulls his hand back. "Funny story, actually. After I got out of prison and hooked up again with some of my old friends, we got wasted one night and they started talking trash about how I was the only ex-con they knew without ink. So I'm not totally clear on the details, but we found one of those all-night tattoo parlors and the next thing I knew, I woke up with this."

"Could've been worse," I say.

"Yeah? How's that?"

I shrug. "You could've ended up with 'Property of Cook County Corrections' inked on your ass."

"You're such a classy girl."

I wink. "I try. Now go buy me some biscuits before I really start to talk dirty and you aren't able to stand up."

He bolts from his seat and I choke on laughter. He turns back and smiles at me and now I know: he's in just as bad as I am. Crap. Crap crap crap crap crap.

Chapter
Fifteen

I'm at Starbucks at the butt crack of dawn on the Sunday morning after Christmas with a Venti double mocha and Kathy in front of me with a blank notebook and the *Big Book*.

"So I assume you understand what the Fourth Step is, even if last time you only half-assed it," she says.

"Excuse me. I fully assed it."

She snorts. "No. You didn't. Because we wouldn't be here if you did. Now, mostly the moral inventory is about resentment, regret, booze, and sex."

"What?" I sputter.

She shrugs. "Well, that's pretty much what it is. You make a list of all the things you resent right now and figure out why that's your problem, and not the problem of the people you resent. You make a list of all the things you regret, now and in the past, then figure out why that's also your problem. Then you make a list of how you dealt with these resentments and regrets with alcohol or sex or both."

"I don't remember them doing it like this in rehab."

Kathy shakes her head. "That's because rehab is meant to dry you out, so you can start to do the real work."

"That sex thing seems sketchy. This isn't Sex Addicts Anonymous."

Kathy flips open the *Big Book* and faces it toward me. "Read this section on the Fourth Step. The whole last bit is all about sexual relationships. Bill W. knew what was what."

If I'm being totally honest, I don't want to get into this with Kathy. Not just because of my less-than-pure thoughts about Joe, but because I'm not sure I want this crusty lady diving through my notes about my sex life. I've worked too damn hard to shut all that down.

"How do you even know if sex was a problem for me?"

She raises an eyebrow. "Sex is a problem for all of us. And you probably more than most. Look at the way you chew gum or smoke cigarettes." She waves to the wrappers of the gum that I've already chewed through since we've been here. "Tell me about your last boyfriend."

"What?"

"Tell me that sex and alcohol weren't all wrapped up together in how that ended—probably how it started too."

I take a sip of coffee. "His name is Brent. And yeah, I guess those were both involved."

"And does he fall into the category of resentment or regret?"

"Don't know. Both, I guess. I resent that I got sent to rehab because I was dropping his wasted ass off."

She scribbles something in the notebook. "And the regret?"

I shrug. I have a world of regret when it comes to Brent but there's no way I'm getting into that with Kathy. "I don't know. I guess I feel bad because I sort of used him. For booze, for someone to party with, whatever."

She nods and scribbles more, then passes the notebook to me. "See? Columns: Regret, Resent, Reason. Now you need to fill in the rest of the list, and include every grudge you're holding on to. Even the ones from a long time ago. Your parents. Your psychiatrist. Whatever. Get them all out. Then we'll meet and talk about it. You'll tell me your story about how you got here and include all the things on the list, and we'll smoke a bunch of cigarettes and then it'll be done."

When I did this in rehab, I had two things I talked about: my parents and school. I didn't mention friends or anything from the past. I didn't mention boxing or Jerry or the gym. I didn't mention the accident or Brent. I didn't want to get into all of that. Steps Four and Five in rehab took two fifty-minute therapy sessions. And I even had some time to kill afterward so we talked about holiday plans.

"You want this for next week?" I say, and then take another piece of gum and shove it into my mouth. The cinnamon flavor goes really well with the mocha.

Kathy snorts. "You won't be able to have a full list by next week, but it'll be a place to start."

I enter my house after the pancake breakfast to a full-on battle. Dad is screaming at Mom to take down all the holiday decorations already and she's bellowing back that it isn't even New Year's yet and she should be allowed to keep them up until then.

I try to slip up to my room, but Dad hears me drop my keys on the table in the front hall. He storms out and stands before me with his hands on his hips.

"You need to start coming to church with us on Sundays."

I blink. "What?"

"We look like we're not a functional family and with all the rumors flying around about your stint in rehab, we need to shore up and have a united front."

I hold my hands up. "What the hell does that mean? Are you listening to yourself? Shore up? Who says shit like that?"

Mom has trailed in behind him and I can tell right away she's been crying.

"Watch your tone, young lady. It's a privilege to be living under my roof, not a right. And I can have you out on your fanny before you even blink."

My mouth drops open. "I . . . I can't go to church. I meet with my sponsor on Sunday mornings and then do my community service."

Dad glares at me, then turns on Mom. "Then none of us go until she can. Until her community service is over. I have more important things to do and I don't want to be fodder for the gossips."

"I want to go to church," Mom says softly.

He shakes his head. "Then you'll go alone. And the decorations come down today. We're done discussing this."

He slams his way upstairs and Mom looks more broken than I've ever seen her. I want to reach out, but I can't imagine she'd want that from me. So instead I say, "Do you need help? I can do the lights outside and the inflatable decorations."

She shakes her head. "I've got it. You've been up since five, why don't you take a nap?"

I make my way upstairs and hear her sniffling as she starts to take the ornaments off the tree, carefully wrapping each in tissue paper.

After five minutes of listening to her, I go to my dresser and grab my workout gear. I pull on my thermals and call to Mom that I'm going for a run before I slam the door and take off.

Running feels fucking terrible. Like I've been living inside an iron lung. But I don't care; I pick up the pace and try not to kill myself on the ice. I do a series of jabs, hooks, and uppercuts when I stop in a park to catch my breath. Then I take off in a sprint again. I used to run miles when I was boxing. I could jump rope for nearly an hour. Mom and Dad didn't even really know. Not until they saw one of my fights. Then it was all concerned looks and discussions about other sports I might be interested in for a while. It wasn't long before it reached ultimatum level.

By the time I get home I'm drenched with sweat and frozen all at the same time. I feel like I've been rolling in the snow. Mom looks at me and shakes her head.

"It would be easier if you didn't smoke so much," she says.

I point to the mountains of decorations she still has to take down in the house. "It would be easier if you didn't decorate so much."

Her bottom lip trembles and she turns away from me. God, I suck as a daughter.

I want to de-stress. I need to. When I get to my room I grab my phone and thumb through my texts to find Brent. But Joe's name is there and on impulse more than anything else, I decide to text him.

I need out or I need to shut off.

My phone rings a second later.

"Where are you?"

"Home."

"What's going on?" I can hear music in the background and figure he must be in his truck.

"I don't want to talk about it. I'm not even sure why I texted you."

He lets out a breath. "You texted because you want to drink

and you want to not drink and you're hoping I'll help you into a more solid place with that."

I laugh. "Are you offering to take me on a bender?"

"If you're going to drink, I'd prefer you were with me, yes. But I'd like a chance to talk to you about why it isn't a good idea, and I need you to tell me why you think it is."

His voice is calm, but my edginess is still slamming into me from all sides. My mom's tears, my dad's concerns about us being a functional family, the way my brain has stopped going blank and seems to actually want me to figure some shit out.

"What's your address?" Joe asks.

"It's 1121 Elmwood. Why?"

"In case you want me to come over."

I'm not sure what to say to this. Or what my parents would think. Asking seems really fucking hard in this moment, but it *is* what I want. The pause is too long between us and I wonder if he's hung up, but knowing Joe, he's waiting on me.

"I'm tired," I start. "I went for a run and I'm tired. But not just from the run. From everything."

"Yeah. You know what they say in AA: Don't HALT. Never be hungry, angry, lonely, or tired."

I laugh a little. "So all four is . . . ?"

"Not great. Do you want me to come over? I can help with two of them. Maybe all four if you don't have to be anywhere this afternoon."

"Can you help with the bender?"

C. Desir

"How about this? How about I come pick you up and talk
to you and if you still want to drink after an hour, I'll take you to
get something to drink?"

I snort. "Enabler."

He laughs. "You haven't heard my pitch yet."

I lie back in my bed and take a deep breath. "There might
be more Tylenol around here somewhere. That could help with
the tired thing."

"I won't come if you don't want me to, but I'd like to."

I let out a long sigh. "You can come."

There's a pause and I guess I should hang up, but I don't.
And neither does he. All that's on the line is our breaths inter-
mingling and the tension of everything I'm not saying crackling
between us.

He clears his throat and says, "Have you ever had the biscuits at Red Lobster? If you think Popeyes is good, you have to
try those Cheddar Bay Biscuits at Red Lobster. Amazing."

"What? What are you talking about?"

"I don't know," he says. "I'm just talking. Keeping you
on the line a little longer so you don't go fishing around for
Tylenol with codeine. Hoping that you'll maybe tell me what's
going on."

"Don't feel like it," I say, and this is the truth. My body is
starting to calm and it'll get worked up again if I talk about
Mom and Dad and the fight and putting on a united front as
a family.

"So then I guess I'll just have to keep talking about biscuits. . . ."

"I need a shower."

"Are you going to take the Tylenol?"

I pause for a second. "No."

"Okay, take your shower. I'll be there soon."

I put the water on as hot as I can get it and let my muscles ease. I used to love showers after a workout. My body is so different now than it was even a year ago. Jesus. Everything slipped away so fast.

I dry off and tug on a big cashmere sweater and Genetic jeans. I eye the medicine cabinet, knowing the Tylenol isn't there anymore, but wondering what else is. Before I can even check, Joe calls.

"I'm in your driveway."

Chapter
Sixteen

Mom says nothing to me when I tell her I'm going out with Joe. She's too wrecked. I shouldn't have said anything about her decorating less. It appears to be the only thing she has control over, which is pretty fucking sad and makes me feel even worse. I should stay with her, but I can't. Not if I want even the slimmest chance of staying sober. I want to explain all this, but it's way too much. So I give her an awkward hug and bolt out the door.

I stand outside the passenger door and Joe rolls down the window.

"Are you waiting for me to open it for you?"

I shake my head. "Hardly. But I do want a guarantee that you'll get me booze if your pitch doesn't work. Promise?"

He narrows his eyes. "Promise you'll listen and have a conversation with me for at least an hour first?"

"Yes," I huff.

"Okay, then yes, I promise. AA pinkie swear or whatever."

I slip into his truck and buckle up. "AA has a pinkie swear?"

"Uh, no. But you can trust me."

I look at my house as he backs out of the driveway. Mom moves robotically around the living room, unwinding lights from the tree.

"Shouldn't you be helping?" Joe says.

"Yeah. That's part of the reason we're going on a bender. Not that you'll be joining me. You're strictly my designated driver."

He turns at the end of my street and steers his truck toward the highway. "You want to get drunk because your mom is taking the lights off the tree?"

"Yeah, something like that."

He waits for me to fill in the rest, but I don't feel up to it. I wait to see what he's going to say next, but he doesn't say anything.

"You now have fifty-four minutes. I thought you were going to give me your pitch."

He rakes his hand through his hair and my gaze catches on the weird symbol tattoos. I wonder if they say "KILL" in Chinese or something. "I thought I'd have a little bit more to work with," he says.

"What do those symbols mean? Did you get them on the *KILL* night too?"

He shakes his head and pulls onto the highway ramp.

"Nah. I got them after. They're Japanese letters."

"What do they spell?"

"Forgiveness," he says.

The air in his pickup grows stifling and I crack my window and pull out a cigarette. "I assume I can smoke."

"Yep."

I go through two of them before either of us says anything. The buzz hits me right away. It must be from the running. Like I cleaned my lungs out enough to start fresh with more death sticks.

Finally, when I can't take the quiet any longer, I say, "Mom is a holiday Nazi. She starts busting out her Christmas sweaters in early November. She has so many ornaments not even our huge tree could hold them all. She loves Christmas. And Dad wanted her to take everything down. They were fighting about it when I got home. Then he told me I needed to go to church with them on Sunday mornings so we'd seem to be more like a functional family."

"Ah."

"Yeah. So I thought maybe I could make that go away."

"The fight?"

"Yeah. It was stupid. But my mom . . . Well, she's had a lot of disappointments lately. She doesn't need to be pummeled when she's already against the ropes."

"And you went running instead of drinking?"

I nod.

"But that didn't help?"

I shake my head and take another drag of my cigarette. "I used to box."

He blinks. "Really?"

"Yeah. I was actually pretty fucking good at it. I started when I was young. Beginning of sixth grade. I went to this gym with my dad. Dad's really into competitive things. And he thought it would be fun bonding. But I don't think he thought I'd get so good or it would be something I was really into."

"Huh. So when did you stop?"

"Almost two years ago. My parents weren't on board for it. And it got to the point where I sort of had to decide if I was going to go all in."

"You started drinking then?"

I shrug. "I drank before that. But not that much. A little bit socially. Boxing training is intense and doing it hungover is fucking awful. And the guy who owns the gym, Jerry, he's a huge hard-ass and pretty unforgiving."

Joe nods. "Did you ever consider it?"

"What?"

"Going all in with boxing."

I swallow. "Yeah," I whisper. "I did. I mean, I quit fighting for a while after my dad told me I needed to find something else. Then I started drinking. Like, really drinking. But there was a time when I thought I'd give up booze and go back to it. Fuck my parents and whoever else said it's not for girls."

"And?"

And I don't want to say anything else, so I shrug. "Shit happens. I never made it back. Well, that's not true, I went back when I was drunk once. Jerry freaked, told me I was pissing away natural talent, that I was a coward."

"There's more to this, isn't there?"

I shake my head. "Not that you need to know. It's just all complicated, is the point. My parents, school, my friends, boxing, drinking, all of it. And when my parents fight, when Mom feels like shit because my dad is a huge asshole, I don't have a lot of options to get rid of the noise. Not anymore anyway."

He gets off the highway and pulls into the Red Lobster parking lot. "There's always going to be noise, Natalie."

"Well, then there's always going to be a reason to drink."

He nods. "Yes. Always. Did you think that would go away? When the physical addiction stuff was over you'd be all set? It doesn't work like that."

I want to rub my eyes. I want to squeeze them shut until they don't sting so much with tears anymore. "Then what is the fucking point? If there's always going to be a reason to drink, why not just drink?"

"The point is you need to learn to deal with noise in a way that doesn't hurt you or other people. You can't make it go away by drinking or shutting off. Because it doesn't go away for good. Just for a little while. And you wake up feeling like crap, not remembering what you did, where you were, what you said, and eventually you destroy everything good in your life just to get rid of noise that will always be there."

He sounds like Kathy and her assurances that things would always be mostly crappy. It's strange how the honesty of this actually makes me feel a bit better. I light another cigarette and slip out of his truck. It's fucking freezing, but I need a little space from this conversation. Joe leans against the pickup on his side and waits. His silence is so annoying I want to flick my cigarette at him to see if that might get a reaction.

"There's no magic pill, Natalie. People who succeed in AA, they know that. It's work. It's a constant struggle. It sucks that it's always going to be that way, but it is. You get comfortable being sober and some new shit happens and you don't want to be sober anymore. But you don't have a choice. You aren't allowed to use the good china anymore. It's paper plates for you from here on out. For all of us."

I blow out a long stream of smoke and put out my cigarette. Before I even realize what I'm doing, I bend over and pick it up and tuck the butt in my box. "And you're fine with that? Fine with using paper plates for the rest of your fucking life when everyone else gets to use the good stuff?"

He nods. "Yes. Because it's not about the plates for me anymore. It's about who I'm having dinner with."

His smile almost breaks me. Almost cracks open the shell and makes everything want to spill out right there on the sidewalk in front of the POS Red Lobster sign. I want to tell him about boxing, about how it really made me feel, about how maybe I wouldn't want to drink if I could have something else. I want to tell him about everything I lost, but I can't say the words. I shake my head and my brain fuses back together. I wasn't supposed to let this guy get to me. And here I am with a thousand questions and way too much hope.

"Let's go. You promised me biscuits," I say, and nudge him toward the front door.

Three biscuits and a plate of shrimp scampi in and the itch to drink has dulled a bit. It's not gone completely, but the shake in my hands is less, and the desire to slam back tequila shots until every part of me goes numb is subsiding.

I'm about to ask Joe about his time in prison when I hear loud voices by the door. Amanda and Amy. Crap. They're laughing and Amy is leaning against the hostess station, and yeah, they're way drunk.

"Oh my God," Amanda says loud enough that several tables turn toward her. Then she grabs Amy and tugs her toward us. "Nattie, what are you doing here? It's soooo good to see you."

We haven't spoken. At all. Not since the afternoon I followed them home. I can feel Joe's gaze on me, but I can't look at him. I'm not up for the reprimand. Amy and Amanda slide into the two empty chairs at our table and I release a loud sigh.

"Amy, Amanda, this is my friend Joe."

Amy leans forward and her eyes are so glazed I think maybe she's on more than just booze.

"Nattie's dating an older guy? Is this why you stopped talking to us?" Amy says, her blond hair falling forward into the basket of biscuits, which . . . gross.

"We're not dating," I say.

"Do you want to get out of here?" Joe says to me in a low voice.

Amanda bursts out laughing. "Oh my God, seriously? You're going to rescue her from us? We're her best friends."

The two of them snort-laugh and I'm sure my face is tomato red. Normally I would be right there with them. Normally I wouldn't sense all the stares or hear the mumbling from the tables around us. But now I do. And I'm embarrassed for them, and for me for having been this way once.

I think again about Camille and the time before I started drinking, when I had normal friends. Friends who cared about me. And I think about how I let them go because I got so into boxing. So obsessed with it. And then I let my boxing friends go because it hurt too much to see them. And for a second I realize that I have always let go of things that are too hard, too much to emotionally deal with. And it has nothing to do with drinking and everything to do with who I am.

My head droops in utter defeat. This is all too hard. I've fucked up almost everything in my life, and the energy required to repair it is too much.

"Hey," Joe says, tapping his fingers on my wrist. "You okay?"

I swallow the lump in my too-dry throat. Now is not the time for revelations. I turn to the A's. "Did you guys drive here?"

Amy shakes her head, then apparently finds it so entertaining she does it over and over until she tilts to the side and starts laughing again. "Brent dropped us off. He's going to meet us here later. I was craving those biscuits." She picks one out of the basket, but doesn't take a bite of it. Just sort of examines it.

"Should I call your parents?" Joe asks, and they both burst out laughing again. Times like this I feel Joe's age. Even sober I would never suggest calling their parents. No one in high school would. It breaks all sorts of unspoken codes of silence.

Plus it wouldn't do any good. Amanda's parents are probably skiing in Aspen—they leave every year after Christmas, and for the past three, they've left her home with her brother. Amy's mom is probably with her latest boyfriend. The only reason she'd care if we called her would be because it interfered with her date. She and Amy are besties of a sort, sharing clothes and gossip and even once a boyfriend, though Amy didn't find out about that until after she'd broken up with him.

"I'll take care of this," I mumble to Joe, and stand up. "Come with me to the bathroom," I tell the A's.

They both stand up, teetering a bit, and stumble after me to the ladies' restroom.

"That guy is so hot. I mean, he probably has an old dick, but he looks like Bradley Cooper," Amy says as soon as we shut the door behind us.

"I know," Amanda says. "Are you on that?"

I shake my head. "No. Of course not. We're friends."

"Oh, come on. The old Nattie would've done him the first night," Amy says. And the thing is, she's probably right. I wouldn't have been sober, but I would've hooked up with him.

I pull out my phone and text Brent.

You need to come pick the girls up now. Are you sober enough to drive?

Thirty seconds later he texts back.

What the hell? I just dropped them off.

Someone's going to call the cops soon. Come get them.

Fine. I'll be there in ten.

I tuck my phone in my back pocket and cross my arms. "The Red Lobster? Really? You show up wasted at the Red Lobster? There are a shitload of families here. You know someone is going to call the cops."

Amy shakes her head. "We're not that wasted. And those biscuits are really good."

Amanda is staring at herself in the mirror. She's leaning forward and back like she's in a fun house.

"Are you on something else?"

Amy giggles. "We might've had a few mushrooms. But only a few."

I roll my eyes. "Jesus, you all are train wrecks."

"Shut up, Nattie. They were your mushrooms. The ones you gave me over the summer that I never took. Stop acting all high-and-mighty."

Amanda snorts. "She can't act all high. Because she can't be high anymore. All the fun has been sucked out of her. And now she's a fun sponge, sucking it out of everyone else."

Amy cackles and the two of them lean against each other as they laugh even harder. This is ridiculous. There's no talking to them. I pull out my phone and text Brent again.

Ping me when you pull up front.

Amy moves next to me and tugs on my hair. She twists her finger around one of the curls and does it for long enough that I realize it's the mushrooms. I bat her hand away.

"We miss you, Nattie," Amy says. "It's not the same when it's just us. We need our third."

"I can't. You know this. My parents would kill me. And I'm on probation."

Amy's lip sticks out. "Will you ever come back to us?"

Her question freezes the breath in my lungs for a second. Because the answer pops in my head so quickly. No hesitation. I'll let go of them like everything else, because it's too hard to be with them. When I was in rehab, I thought it was about waiting. Doing my time until I was eighteen, off probation, in college. It wasn't about quitting, it was about putting off drinking and partying until I could take it up again. But somehow now, with Joe, with Kathy, with all the old alkies at SFC, it's different.

"No," I say. "I won't."

And even as I say it, the itchiness seeps out of me. Because letting go of this is the right thing to do. The need to shut off the noise dissipates and all I want now is to go sit back down with Joe and eat biscuits and talk about stupid things and important things and know that for some reason, he's decided I'm worth this.

There's a knock at the door just as my phone pings with Brent's *I'm here* text.

"Everything okay, Natalie?"

I pull the door open and nod at Joe. "Their ride is here. Sorry I left you alone like that."

He searches my face and looks past me to the A's. Then he nods. "No problem. Need help?"

Amy waves her hand. "We've got it, Romeo. Thanks for the concern, but we can manage all on our own."

Then she and Amanda push past me and teeter toward the door. We should probably follow Brent's car, make sure they make it home, but I'm so tired.

"You can't save everyone," Joe says, and steers me back to the table. "Especially when they have no interest in being saved."

"I didn't have any interest in being saved."

He shrugs. "Yes, you did."

I shake my head. "No. I didn't."

He plucks a fresh biscuit out of the basket and puts it on my plate. "Of course you did. You wouldn't have come back otherwise. You wouldn't have called me an hour and a half ago. You wouldn't be here right now."

"I had to come back. Court ordered."

He pauses then and taps my wrist again. "What happened? Something's wrong. Something more than your drunk friends."

I gnaw at my lip for a second, then say, "How do you know the difference between letting go of something because it's too hard and letting go of something because it's the right thing to do?"

"Are we talking about them?" He waves in the direction of the door.

"Yes. No. Sort of. I don't know. I just think that I always walk away when things get to be too much and maybe I shouldn't. Maybe I should live with it."

He nods. "Well, that's true. If you bail because it's getting tough, then you'll never learn to deal with anything. But sometimes we have to walk away because it's the best thing for us. And maybe it's hard and maybe it's easy, but in the end, it's still the best thing for us."

"I don't know what's best for me. It's not how I work. I

work on a feel-good spectrum. If it feels good, then I'm in. If it doesn't, I bail."

He shakes his head. "Don't sell yourself short. I've spent enough time with you to know you're not that shallow. You know what's best for you. Now eat your biscuit and tell me how far along you are with Kathy."

Chapter
Seventeen

"**Did you make your list?**" Kathy asks as soon as I slide into the plush velvet Starbucks chair across from her.

I kick my feet up onto the table and take a long sip of coffee. "Yeah. It's done."

Kathy shakes her head. "No. It's not. But let's hear what you've got so far."

I take another sip. "No 'good morning, Natalie.' No 'you made it on time,' just right to the list, huh?"

"Good morning, Natalie. Did you go to all your meetings this week?"

"I talked to you yesterday. You know I went to all my meetings."

She pulls off a bite of scone and pops it in her mouth. "That's right. We talked four times this week. And every single time, you didn't say anything about the Fourth Step or your list. So. We're here to work and I want to know what you've got so far."

I take a deep breath, suddenly nervous. I jotted down a few things, but I kept getting tripped up on the past regrets thing. And on the sex thing. You start looking at your life in terms of the guys you've had drunken hookups with and things get real depressing real fast.

I pull out a piece of yellow lined paper I got from my dad's office and stare at it for a few seconds. "I resent my parents. They want me to be a certain way. I'm inconvenient for them and that sort of pisses me off."

Kathy nods. "Yeah. That's probably a big one. Did you think about whether or not that's something you have control over?"

"What do you mean?"

She leans forward and her boobs droop low, pressing against her button-down shirt. I hope my body never gets old like this. "I mean, think about the Serenity Prayer. Half the reason people drink is because they're worked up over things they have no control over. So every time you start getting worked up, you got to put up a mental block that stops you and reminds you to focus back on what you can control."

"I can't control anything."

I'm not sure I mean to say this, but as soon as it slips out, it feels an awful lot like truth. Like every time I want something so bad, I never get it. And there's always so much disappointment. And that's probably the reason I let go of stuff when it starts to get hard, because I'm so fucking sick of disappointment.

"You can control things," Kathy says. "You can control your

choices. You can control how you choose to react to others."

"In the grand scheme of things, that doesn't feel like very much."

"Exactly," she says, sipping from her coffee. "And the minute you realize how little control you have over things, it all gets easier. We've talked about this before. There's nothing you can do about other people and their shit. You have to mind your own business, do your work, trust God, and help others."

The God thing continues to be a bit of a holdup for me. Even growing up in a pretty progressive church, I feel conflicted about faith. Kathy knows it too. She keeps on focusing on the agnostic stuff in AA because she knows I'm not a full believer. There are just too many holes in most religions and too many people using religion as an excuse to be an asshole. But I'm not quite the skeptic I was when I left rehab. And if I'm being completely honest, it's because Joe and Kathy haven't let me down. Which maybe doesn't really equate to any kind of higher power, but I've let Kathy draw me into those discussions because *she* thinks Joe and her were put in my life by God.

"I get that I can't control my parents, but it might be nice if they did me a solid every once in a while and stepped up to the plate to actually parent."

Kathy snorts. "What do you think rehab was for? What do you think that Breathalyzer on your car is for? The world doesn't revolve around you. There's only one God and you aren't it."

"Way to hit me with the tough love, Kath. Is this how you get all young alkies to keep coming back?"

"Hardly. But you're a brat and you need to get your head out of your ass and own your shit. You got money, you got a mom who cares enough about you to send you to rehab, you're young, and you got a lot of options for the future. Look at the life that's laid out before you. You can take all these winning lottery tickets you've been handed and cash them in, or you can go get drunk and piss everything away. You're a lot luckier than most of us. When I hit rock bottom, my choice was a halfway house or living on the street. I'd lost my husband, my job, my home."

I don't want to feel like this. I don't want to feel bad because my life is better than Kathy's. It isn't my fault. "This sounds like stuff I have no control over."

It's a bitchy thing to say and I know it, but Kathy doesn't lash out like I expect her to. "You're absolutely right. And it's not my sharing time, it's yours. So what else do you have on that list of yours?"

"I resent Mrs. Hunt. She's one of my teachers who's been riding me to get all my assignments made up."

Kathy nods. "You should be making them up. That's your job. That's something you can control."

"I'm under a lot of pressure right now."

"Oh, cry me a river. You want to know pressure? Try having your ex, who you love more than anyone, show up and ask you if you want to get back together, which is incredible, only you know saying yes will put you right back in that place of wanting to drink. All the time. And saying no feels like it will carve the inside of your heart into pieces and you may never recover from that."

"Whoa." I sit back and stare at her. "So. This *is* about some shit you have going on."

"No." She waves a hand. "Sorry. I shouldn't have said all that. It's sort of spilling over into all parts of my life."

"Have you talked to your sponsor?"

She nods. "Yeah. An hour a day for the past week."

"You really love your ex? And he wants to get back with you?"

"Yeah. But it's really complicated."

I shrug and take a sip of coffee. "Well, seeing as I've already covered you off on the two things on my list, you can take a turn if you want."

Kathy's head tilts. "Huh. Look at you. Trying to help people."

I grin. "Don't get me wrong. The world still revolves around me. But since you happen to be in my life, I'm willing to let the spotlight wander onto you for a while."

"So generous," she says, then sighs. "Do you know my ex is Joe's brother?"

I nod. "Yeah. He told me."

"Figured. He doesn't talk to Joe anymore. I didn't think he'd ever talk to me again either."

Whoa. Again I'm surprised. I thought Joe had all his steps locked, but now I wonder how much is a front and if maybe Joe isn't as together as I thought.

She shakes her head and gives me a pathetic look. "I honestly don't know what I'm going to do."

I stare at her but she doesn't say anything else. I feel like I should probably have some words of wisdom, but I don't know shit. So instead I go back to talking about Mrs. Hunt and school, which is weak sauce, but Kathy doesn't seem to mind.

Monday at school, Camille invites me to sit with her and her friends at lunch. I'm not even sure what to do with this and I barely say a word to her until almost the end of the period.

"How come you asked me to sit with you?" I finally blurt out before shoving a large bite of sandwich into my mouth.

She shrugs. "You seem lonely. You're always sitting with the burnouts, but you don't talk to them, and I know you're trying to stay sober."

I nod. I should say something. Apologize. Or make amends or what-the-fuck-ever I'm supposed to do here. But I can't.

"You're welcome, Nat," she says, and then turns back to her friends.

Alex is at the meeting on Monday afternoon. He raises his eyebrows when I walk in and pats the seat beside him, but I take a different one across the room. He is persistent, I'll give him that. As I'm watching the clock, waiting for the leader to stop chatting and start the meeting, I think about Kathy. I still feel weird about everything she let slip on Sunday. I gather she and her ex have a really tumultuous past and I'd be as worried as she is if I were in that place. And the fact that he and Joe don't talk makes me wonder how far Joe really fell before he got sober.

It also makes me again think maybe I don't belong here. Maybe the problem isn't alcohol, it's me. And there's no undoing that in twelve steps.

Joe slides in next to me just as the old bald leader with shaky hands starts the meeting. "Good afternoon, everyone. My name is Stan and I'm an alcoholic."—"Hi, Stan"—"This is the four thirty closed meeting of Alcoholics Anonymous . . ."

Alex stands outside with us after the meeting, smoking menthols. He looks at me too close and I have an urge to hide behind Joe.

"What'd you do for New Year's, baby girl? Stay sober?" Alex asks, taking a step closer to me.

"Yeah, actually. I finished up some of my school assignments and then met Kathy for dinner."

Mom wanted to stay in and do a romantic-comedy movie marathon, but Jesus fucking Christ, there's only so much I can take of pretend family bonding. And it's not like any of my friends were knocking on my door to hang out.

"You got to call me next time you want to go out to eat, beautiful. I'm way more fun than Kathy. Even sober," Alex says, and winks at me.

"How was your New Year's, Alex? Did you go for a drive?"

Joe asks, and immediately something in Alex's face shuts down.

"Just fine, *cabrón*. Yours?"

Joe inhales and nods. "Good. Went to a meeting. Caught a movie."

Alex lights another cigarette. I notice he's dropped his first and left it on the ground. I'm waiting for Joe to lean down and pick it up but he doesn't move. "Sounds like fun. Hope you didn't get an upset stomach from the popcorn. That happens to my dad. He says it happens to all old guys."

Joe blinks. I step between them because whatever kind of bullshit posturing is going on here, I feel compelled to break it up.

"What'd you do for New Year's, Alex?" I ask.

Alex flinches and I realize I've said something wrong. But then just as fast, his face softens and he smiles at me. "Nothing, *querida*. I got a brother who died on New Year's, so my family went to his grave site."

"I'm so sorry," I say. His eyes look sad and haunted and I don't want to push, but I wonder what the story is here. And how Joe seems to know it.

"It's okay," Alex says, then moves forward to tuck one of my curls behind my ear.

Joe grabs my arm and pulls me closer to him. "Alex . . ." The warning is as clear as day.

Alex laughs and drops his cigarette. "I don't know what you think you've got going on with this girl, Joe, but she's too much for you to handle. And too young. She needs a man her own age."

"Too bad there aren't any men her own age around. Just boys," Joe answers.

I blink. "Are you kidding me with this? You're measuring your dicks because of me? No. I don't think so. I don't want any part of this. Whatever shit is going on between you two has nothing to do with me."

I drop my cigarettes back into my purse and head toward where my car is parked. Alex calls out after me, but I ignore him. I slide into the driver's seat and take three deep breaths. I'm about to breathe into the tube to get the car started when Joe taps on my window.

I open the door and peer up at him. "What the hell was that about?"

"I told you. Alex goes after girls who come through AA. He's given at least one an STD."

"I wasn't trying to date him. I was having a conversation. I was showing sympathy for his situation with his brother. What the hell? Isn't that what I'm supposed to do? Help others."

"His brother died in a car crash while Alex was driving him home drunk."

I gasp. "Jesus. Really?"

He nods.

"You're a dick for bringing it up," I say. He flinches, and I know I'm right. Even if Alex is responsible for that, there's no need to pour salt in those wounds. He's probably beating himself up more than anyone else could.

Joe lets out a long breath. "Can I just talk to you for a minute?"

I nod and he comes to the passenger side and gets in. I raise an eyebrow at him and he rakes his fingers through his hair. Neither of us speaks for several seconds.

"You're right. It was a dick move. It's just . . . I don't know what I'm doing with you," he says finally.

So he's ready to put it out there. Which I guess shouldn't surprise me, because AA is so much about being honest with yourself and others. But the thing is, I'm not ready for it. I know I want him. I've wanted him for a while. But I can't tell how much of it is real and how much of it is that he's there in a way no one has been for me. Plus *he* wants me, which I like and want because it makes me feel like I'm worth something. Which maybe isn't the best reason to start this conversation. My ambivalence over all the layers is what keeps stopping me from saying or doing anything.

"You're being a friend," I say, and reach out to squeeze his hand, because that's the best I can do.

He shakes his head. "I don't feel this way about my friends. I don't have this instinct to protect them like I do with you."

I give a sort of sad laugh because it's everything I crave for probably all the wrong reasons. "I guess I'm special then."

He takes my hand between his two and it feels so good and so confusing all at once. I want to hop into his lap and make out with him. But I want to be drunk to get to that place. Like somehow if I'm drunk all these things I'm feeling will be okay.

All this want would make sense if we were just fooling around while we were high and it wasn't a big deal. But it *is* a big deal. He's a lot older than me. I'm newly sober. He's an ex-con, and I'm supposed to be applying for college or figuring out what the hell to do with my life. There are a million things wrong with this. And this is hardly the easy path.

"You *are* special, Nat."

It's too much. How he's looking at me and how my heart is beating and how I can't stop staring at his mouth and wondering what he'd taste like, if he's a good kisser, what his hands would feel like.

"You should go," I whisper, and he lets out a long sigh. Almost like relief.

"I should." He squeezes my hand once more and drops it. Then he opens his door and slides out of the car. "Talk to Kathy. She can help more than I can at this point."

I nod but don't say anything else. He doesn't know about his brother or what Kathy's going through, and it's not my place to tell him. They obviously have some sort of history and I'm not about to get involved with that.

I breathe into the tube to get the car started, then make my way home, thinking the entire time about my hand sandwiched between Joe's and how I didn't really want him to let go.

That night I slip downstairs into our basement gym and work out hard. I even have a go at the punching bag, but I'm too rusty and my arms start to hurt after five minutes. Mom comes down and watches me for a while.

"Do you miss it?" she asks.

"What?"

"Boxing."

I shrug. "You don't want that kind of daughter."

She shakes her head. "We never should've asked you to pull back. We lost you after that."

"I'm right here."

"Lost," she says again, then after a pause, "You could go back."

"It's too late. I'm not in any kind of shape for it. I'm not good enough."

"Jerry says you're good enough."

I pause my bicep curls and stare at her. "When did you talk to Jerry?"

"He called a few weeks ago asking about you. He didn't want you to know, but I'm tired of all the secrets and lies. He asked if you were really sober."

"Why is that Jerry's business?"

She stands and crosses the room to me. She grabs the towel folded on the treadmill and hands it to me. "Because he thinks you have talent. He thinks you could do this, if you really wanted it. You're not too old to start training for the amateur circuit. You'd need to work hard, but . . ."

I drop the weight at my feet and hold my hands up. "Don't

pretend this is okay with you. That you'd be fine with a fucking boxer as a daughter. Dad made himself perfectly clear on that score two years ago. 'Our kind don't box professionally.'"

She shakes her head. "Do you really want this?"

Tears press against my eyes and I can't speak. I can't have this. I've been resigned to it. I gave it up, let it go. All the signs told me no, it wasn't for me. I dig deep and bury the hope her words spark in me. Then I wrap the towel around my neck and leave her standing in the basement alone.

Chapter
Eighteen

It's two o'clock in the morning and I'm woken by thumps on my window. I peek out and of course it's Brent with a handful of rocks from the rock garden at the end of our driveway. Rocks, not pebbles. What an idiot.

I pull open the window and hiss down to him, "Stop. You'll wake my parents. I'm coming down."

There's no point trying to get him to go away. He's obviously drunk and on some sort of mission. I pull the front door open and he's leaning against the side of my house.

"Two a.m. Really? This is the house you come to after boozing all night?"

He grins, but his gaze is glassy. Definitely drunk. "I wanted to talk to you. School starts again in two days, and I want to clear some stuff up. You've been avoiding it long enough."

I sigh. "And you couldn't stop by tomorrow?"

He tilts to the side when he shakes his head. "No. Now."

I roll my eyes, but pull him inside, whispering, "You have to be quiet. My parents have their white noise machine on, but they'll hear stumbling and loud voices."

He nods and grabs for my hand. I let him keep it in his grasp, if only to make sure he stays steady as he follows me to my room. When we get there, I shut the door and fold my arms, leaning against the wall as he stumbles toward the bed and lies down with a moan.

"Your bed is so soft," he says.

"Mom put a feather bed on top."

He rolls to his side and smiles at me. "Your mom takes care of you."

I shrug.

"That's good. Someone should take care of you."

My arms tighten across my body. "Did you want to tell me something? Because I'd like to get this over with so I can go back to sleep like normal people."

He reaches out and waves me closer to him. I take a few steps, but stop before I get too close. "You used to be awake at this time," he says. "You used to party later than any of us. I've never seen someone get by on so little sleep."

"I slept. Just mostly during the day on weekends."

He grins. "Yeah."

"So?"

"Do you remember that night?" he says, and suddenly he sounds a lot more sober than he did a few minutes ago.

"The night you drove me home and got your DUI."

Every part of me is tensing. I've been avoiding this for weeks, and even now with Brent in front of me, my brain is starting to fuzz out and push my thoughts away. "Of course I remember that night. You were wasted. I got a DUI. The end."

He shakes his head and rolls onto his back, staring at my ceiling. The silence between us lasts long enough for me to wonder if he's maybe fallen asleep, which would be fricking perfect. But then he releases a long sigh.

"Do you remember what you told me at the beginning of the party? After you'd already had a few shots?"

He's going at it head-on. There's going to be no way out of this, but still I try. "No. It was months ago."

"You want to know why I got so drunk after?"

"No. I don't. I don't want to talk about this. You need to get out of here. My parents—"

"Are you just going to pretend, Nattie? Be all breezy about it, same as you were that night?"

"Oh, fuck off, Brent. There's nothing to pretend. It's irrelevant. I can't even believe you're bringing it up."

He sits up and holds himself steady for a second, like maybe the room is spinning. "I can't believe you won't talk about it. I keep trying. And you keep shutting me down."

"Get out. For real. Get the fuck out of here before I scream and my parents call the cops."

Brent rises and shakes his head. "So this is it? You're not going to let me—"

I flap my arms at him. "Stop. Get out. Now. I'm serious."

He heaves a sigh and stumbles to the door. I follow him downstairs and realize I'm probably going to have to drive him home. But when he exits the front door, he starts walking down the street. No car. Thank God for that at least. It's freezing and I should probably offer him a ride, but I don't want to continue this conversation. I don't want to answer his questions. I don't want to think about that night or what I told him. I thought I might be ready for it, but I'm not. I'm nowhere near ready. I want it all to pour out of my head like it never happened, but my brain isn't working in my favor now. It's like a cat with a mouse. Which means there's really only one choice for me.

"Where did you get the vodka, Natalie?"

Mom's harsh voice breaks through the fracture in my brain. I crack open an eye and immediately shut it. I'm slightly buzzed still and it's too bright.

"Answer your mother." Dad. Great.

"Twenty-four-hour Walgreens."

"Do you have a fake ID? Let me have it."

I roll onto my back but keep my eyes shut. "No. No fake ID. There's just a really friendly cashier guy who works nights there."

"Thank Christ I put that Breathalyzer on her car. I can only imagine the type of scene she'd have made if she got pulled over for another DUI. The neighbors would never stop talking about it." Dad again. Part of me wonders if I should care that the neighbors' gossip is really the only important thing to him, but my brain hurts too much to think about it. He's Dad. That's how he rolls.

"I think you should call your sponsor," Mom says now. "Tell her about your slip. Get back on the program."

My *slip*. Yes. That's how Mom would see it. Like all I need to do is dust myself off and start working the steps again, when really all I can think about is having an orange-juice-and-gin breakfast drink to take the edge off the pounding in my head. To forget my mom's mention of Jerry. To forget Brent's visit. To forget that this is my life.

"I'll call her later. I need a few more hours of sleep," I say.

Dad huffs. "Clean her up, Sarah. We're not going through all this again." Then I hear his footsteps and my door shutting. It sounds like a slam, but it could be my head.

I slit my eyes open again and glance at Mom's face. Tearstains on her cheeks and red eyes. I'm horrible, but I don't have the energy to make this right. Instead I say, "I'll call Kathy as soon as I get up. Promise. I just need a few more hours . . ."

"You have thirty minutes," she says, tilting her chin slightly so I know she's going to be firm on this. "Then I'm coming back in here to wake you up and get you in the shower."

I wave at her and she turns away, tiptoeing toward the door and opening and shutting it softly behind her. It's considerate. I know she is trying to give me a break. I also know, as my eyes flutter closed again, that neither of my parents asked why I was drinking in the first place.

Chapter
Nineteen

Kathy's waiting for me at the Starbucks. Her eyes narrow as she gazes at my face.

"You missed your sponsor meeting this morning. And community service. Left Joe in the lurch for the pancake breakfast."

I raise a shoulder. "I'm here, aren't I?"

"Do you want to be?"

Well, that *is* a legit question. Much better than anything Mom has said to me so far today.

"I don't know," I answer.

"Fair enough. Wanna tell me what happened?"

I shake my head. "Not really."

"Natalie, no one expects you to be perfect. Mistakes, relapses, slip-ups, they come with the territory. I don't know anyone who quit drinking that ever cold turkeyed it without making one mistake. But there's a big difference between fucking up and knowing you're an alcoholic and need to try again, and fucking up because you don't think you have a problem. So which is it?"

I pull out my cigarettes with shaky hands. I can't smoke inside, but I need the feel of the box, as much as I need to ignore the six texts from Joe waiting on my phone.

"I have a problem," I whisper.

Kathy nods. "Yeah, you do. Now. You want to tell me what happened?"

This is part of the Fifth Step. I know if I start to tell her everything, it's all going to tumble out of me and spill into the space between us. And part of me isn't ready for that. Not with Kathy. Not when . . .

Her phone pings and she glances down. A flash of anger and something else crosses her face. Maybe hope?

"Your ex?" I ask.

She nods. "I told him I needed time to think. He's respected that, but he calls or texts every day. I think he wants me to know he's committed. I'm stupid for even hesitating. I'm the one who hurt him. I'm the alcoholic. This should be a dream come true, him wanting me back."

"But . . . it's not?"

"Like I said, it's complicated. That's all. It's hard to live with someone who has seen the shittiest part of you. It's hard to live with someone you hurt so much, because you're constantly reminded of your past mistakes. You know more people break up after they get sober than before. The rate of divorce in recovering alcoholics is really high. Part of it might be resentment, but I think part of it is the difficulty of being with someone who has seen you at your worst."

Which sort of decides it for me. Kathy can't be the person I spill everything to. She's not the "other human being" in my Fifth Step: *Admitted to God, to ourselves, and to another human being the exact nature of our wrongs.* My stuff is ridiculous in comparison. Even I'm rolling my eyes at how stupid it would all sound to her.

"Yeah, that's hard," I agree. "Well, look, I don't mean to bail on you, but I sort of owe Joe an apology and I thought I'd go do that."

She blinks and I can see she's still distracted, which is maybe why she says, "Okay. But show up next week. Call me tomorrow. Relapses don't have to be the end of it. You can shake this off."

I nod and get up, grabbing my box of cigarettes. "Yeah. I know. Call your ex. He seems like a good guy."

I don't actually know. He could be a douche, but the smile she gives me makes me think probably not. She's looking for permission with him and if I can give her that, then that's a good thing, I guess.

"Why didn't you call?" Joe asks as he pours me a cup of coffee and slides it in front of me.

This is the first time I've been to his place, which is actually a small trailer, only like no other trailer I've ever seen. It's clean and sort of eco-fancy. Like I'm probably leaning on a counter made of recycled materials and the coffee was probably made using energy from the solar paneling on the roof.

My hand slides along the counter and up to the cast iron pots hanging on the wall. "You don't have a lot of stuff," I say, noting how perfectly everything fits into this small space. There's a section that's walled off at the end of the trailer, which I assume is where his bed is.

"No. I don't need much."

"Did you build this place?"

"Mostly. I had a guy help me with the electrics and some of the carpentry. But, yeah, I built it. I got the idea from an architect I know. She was trying to get out from under a mountain of messy divorce debt. She didn't want a house payment anymore. So she got a flatbed trailer and built herself a house for less than twelve grand. Sort of amazing, really."

"It's small," I say, twisting my hands in front of me. The space between Joe and me seems almost nonexistent. I'm hyper-aware of every move he's making and I'm sure he's equally aware of me. I can almost feel his breath on my cheek.

"It's just me living here," he says.

Silence sits between us, but it's not the usual comfortable silence of being with Joe. It's his waiting silence.

"I didn't call because I wanted to drink," I finally say. "So I powered off my phone and got some vodka instead."

"Yeah, I got that part." He steps even closer to me and steers me toward the tiny table at the end of the counter. I sit and he slips into the chair opposite.

"I can't do my Fifth Step with Kathy."

His brow furrows. "Why not?"

I shake my head. He doesn't know about his brother. Still. And telling him is going way past oversharing into crossing boundaries I don't want to get involved with. "It's not my place to say. But she's not in a good spot to help me with it."

"I talked to her this morning when you didn't show up. She seems fine."

"Look. You need to let it go. I don't want to tell her all my shit. Whether that's because of her or me is irrelevant. The point is, I'm not getting into it all with her."

"You have to do it with someone," he says.

I nod and look at him, searching his face for permission, for some sort of sign he understands what I'm feeling. "I can't do it with Kathy. I can't," I say again.

He reaches across the table and takes my hand. "I won't be that person for you, Natalie. It's too . . . loaded. You know that."

I do, but it doesn't change how I feel. "You're the only one I could tell," I blurt out. "You're the only one who I think could know my whole truth and not judge me for it."

He shakes his head. "We can't . . ."

"I'm not looking for epic love, Joe. All I want, all I really need, is someone who gives a shit about my story. Someone who cares enough to listen."

The words are like pieces of me being pried from my body. I can't believe I've even said them. I have no idea how I got to this place from where I was last night. All I know is that I need him with a strange desperation. I *need* him. To listen and say it's okay and hold my hand and tell me that I'm going to make it and that maybe I'm not the worst person in the world.

"Please," I whisper. "I won't get through it without you."

The whole atmosphere in the room has changed. And I'm almost one hundred percent certain he's going to turn me away, send me home, back to the darkness.

"Okay," he says at last. "Okay."

Chapter
Twenty

Joe stands to get an ashtray. It's one of those smokeless kinds, which is maybe why his tiny eco-trailer doesn't smell like cigarettes. I pull my pack from my purse and light one before I say anything.

"So how does it work?"

"Well," he says, lighting his own cigarette, "there's no specific way. You can tell me how it was going through your moral inventory, what you figured out about yourself. Or you can tell me your story, weaving your moral inventory into it."

"Kathy told me it's mostly about sex."

Joe doesn't flinch but his hand shakes the tiniest bit as he flicks an ash. "Depends. It can be. It isn't for everyone."

"Was it for you?"

He stares at me for a second and I'm worried I've already pushed too hard. Finally he says, "Yes and no. But this isn't my Fifth Step, it's yours. I'll answer your questions, but you and I both know that's just you stalling. So. Why don't you tell me what happened last night?"

I take a full drag. "No. I need to back up to before then."

He nods.

"It's not like I didn't know about my addictive personality. I mean, I've always sort of been an all-or-nothing kind of girl. But I didn't really think it would happen with drinking. I mean, everyone in high school drinks, right?"

"Not everyone."

I wave the hand holding my cigarette. "I'm not talking about the athletes in training or the losers who never go to parties. I'm talking about most people. And it's not just my circle. I bet at least three-quarters of my class have had a drink. Most of them probably had one by freshman year. Before I had loadie friends, I had regular friends and they all drank some, even the ones on the honors track. It's how things are these days."

Joe blinks. "These days?"

"Fuck off. I'm not calling you old. I'm just saying that most people at my high school have had a drink. And probably most people in any high school. It's what teenagers do. And access is pretty easy."

"Okay. So, you've been drinking since . . . ?"

I inhale deeply on my cigarette and end up coughing. "I had my first drink in sixth grade. It was at one of my parents' parties. But it wasn't a big deal. And that was the year I first started boxing."

Joe smiles and part of me melts a little, but I shore up my defenses.

"So I didn't drink much because I boxed. And you know how I told you I got good after a few years, like really good, but my parents didn't want me to do it."

He nods. "And?"

"And I gave it up for a while—the boxing—and started drinking a lot more. Because if I didn't, I think I probably would've ended up beating the crap out of everyone. The thing about boxing isn't just that I was good. It was that it belonged to me, you know? No one else does it. I mean, yeah, girls do it, but no one from my school, no one my parents know. It was all mine."

"But you gave it up."

I look up for a second. "Yeah. Because my parents told me to. They kept on me about it, telling me it could only be a hobby. Complaining about my bruises and how I didn't look like other girls. Making it hard for me to keep going. And I always fucking give up things that are too hard. But I missed it so much that after a while, I figured, fuck my parents, I'm going to get sober and do it anyway. But it was like everything was stacked against me, you know? It wasn't just having to quit drinking, which at that point, I figured I probably could. It was . . ."

I can't finish. There's a roadblock in the back of my throat that won't let me finish that line of thought, so I change direction. "By the beginning of last year I was drinking every day. My friends and I would take water bottles of powdered orange drink and vodka to school every morning. I think they added water too. I did at first, but by May it was just the vodka and the orange powder."

I expect Joe to say something about me refusing to believe I was the same as all the other alkies when I first started AA, but he doesn't. He waits and lets me pull together my story. It's so easy with him.

"I didn't think it was that big a deal, is the thing. Because my friends were doing it with me. And yeah, I was drinking more. Drinking at home alone sometimes. Starting my weekends with V8 and vodkas. Not remembering parts of the nights when I'd go out and party."

"And you didn't get the DTs when you were in rehab?" Joe asks.

I shake my head. "No. Maybe because I'm young. Maybe because it hadn't been going on for ten years like the other alkies. I don't know. I wanted to drink. I still do. Like I would peel off my own skin to be having this conversation over shots right now. But it's not all I want."

"So it's not just rehab that got you to quit?"

I shrug. "Well, the court situation didn't help. And you know my dad installed a Breathalyzer on my car."

"Natalie. I've been there. If you're at the peel-your-skin-off-for-a-drink stage, that's pretty far gone. Court cards and a car Breathalyzer aren't much of a deterrent. You proved that last night. So what was it? What did it? What made you at least want to try to quit for good? Because this is hard, and you told me that you don't hold on to things that are too hard. So why are you holding on to sobriety?"

I'm lighting my second cigarette as I say, "You trying to figure out my rock bottom? What pushed me to the point that I actually want to stay sober? I don't know. I don't think I have a real defining moment. No 'Hey, Nat, get your shit together' come to Jesus. Staying sober is hard, but so is being drunk. That's why I'm not the same as you."

"Not everyone hits rock bottom like that. Sometimes we just wake up and realize we're pretty broken and the only way out of the hole is up."

"Are we already to that part of the half hour? The platitudes about working the program and believing in my higher power? You don't even want me to tell you about my crappy childhood or give you my poor-little-rich-girl sob story?"

He doesn't even smile. "Why do you do that?"

"What?"

"Why do you make it seem like you're not worth anything? Like your problems aren't important?"

"Because they're not. There are people starving in the world. People who have to live on the streets. People who grew up with single moms living on welfare."

He reaches across the table and covers my hand with his.

"Natalie. These things don't change how we feel. They don't change the holes inside us. They don't change our addictions."

"But it's all stupid. My current problems exist because I drink. I made this crappy bed that I now have to lie in."

"Maybe. Or maybe you started drinking to make your problems go away, and what really happened was they ended up just getting worse. Maybe your drinking was more about avoiding the hard stuff."

I shrug and release a stream of smoke. The smokeless ashtray doesn't work that well, I'm noticing, which makes me think maybe Joe doesn't smoke inside that often.

"Should we go outside to smoke?"

"No," he says. "It's freezing outside and I'm not going to sit out there for hours while you spill your life story just to prevent a lingering smoke smell. It'll be fine."

"It won't take me hours to tell my story."

He looks at the clock on his wall. "Thirty minutes so far and all you've really said is that you're good at boxing and you had a crappy childhood. But you haven't explained what that part means."

I sigh. "Oh, you know. The same as everyone else. It was fine. I'm an only child. My parents' pride and joy. Except that's maybe not so true anymore. And I'm not sure how true it's ever been. Maybe with Mom. But I think that has more to do with the fact that she doesn't have a job, so there's nothing she can call her own beyond her role as wife and mother. But it's always been wife first. My dad is sort of a big shot at the Board of Trade."

Joe nods. "And your mom has never worked?"

"She did before she had me. She worked at the library. But then I was a difficult baby—they remind me of this often—and I guess Mom couldn't really leave me with a babysitter for very long. She was sort of this crazy breast-feeder and I wouldn't ever take the bottle. My dad was mortified about the whole thing, but she held her ground. I don't know. It was a long time ago. And when I started eating real food, Dad got her back and turned her into this amazing trophy-wife hostess."

Joe raises his eyebrow at this. "She doesn't seem like a tro-phy wife."

"Well, not in that boob-job, plastic-surgery kind of way, but believe me, she has mad skills when it comes to taking up no space so there's plenty of room for the ego of Dad and all his trader buddies. You should see her when she's hosting. It's like she asks all the right questions, gets people to share their completely vapid life stories, without saying one thing about herself. From the outside, she has the emotional landscape of a rock garden."

Joe laughs. "Well, rock gardens can be pretty elaborate if you're serious about the design."

I light a third cigarette. "Yes, but they seem like noth-ing on the outside. That's Mom. She's so good at faking—at lying, really—that you'd never really know how unhappy she is unless you were in her shoes."

"How do you know?"

"Because I live with him too. Because he told me to give up boxing and she didn't fight for me. And now . . . she says maybe I could have it back, but I just know he won't let me. And asking for it, wanting it, that seems really hard."

"Yes, probably it will be. Especially if your dad doesn't want it for you."

I nod. "Nothing else matters to him but what it looks like from the outside. That's why my boxing, my DUI, my rehab, even going to AA meetings is a huge fucking inconvenience for him. And he orders Mom around like she has no brain, like she can't pull off the simplest of tasks when she's been holding our family together forever."

"So. This is resentment. Which must have been on your list. And now we're going to cross it off. And you're going to let this go."

"I am?"

"Yes," he says. "Because this is something, someone, you have no control over. Your dad has made his choices. They aren't the choices you would make. Same with your mom. But they don't belong to you. There is nothing you can do to change them. It isn't your responsibility. You want people to be better, but that can't be on you. The only person you can make better is you."

"Does that mean that I should just stand on the sidelines watching as he continues to treat my mom like shit? As he continues to get mad that I'm not everything he wants me to be?"

"No. You should tell him, tell them both, how you feel. Because that's your truth. Because you're allowed to make your own choices. But you shouldn't expect them to change or suddenly support you. That choice is theirs to make alone. You're not the hall monitor for better behavior in parents. It doesn't work that way. Their system of dysfunction has been working for them for a long time, I'm guessing. You can choose not to be party to it, but you can't pull the whole system out from under them if they want to hold on to it. Let go of this resentment. Be honest with them. Be honest with yourself. But this can't belong to you anymore."

The softness of his voice is my undoing. My body starts to itch and I stand up and walk to the end of the trailer, turn, come back, walk it again.

"Why are you being nice to me?" I ask after my third rotation.

"Because everyone needs help. Everyone needs someone to care about their stories."

He's turning my words inside out and it makes me start to shake. I don't deserve this. I don't deserve him spending his time listening to me. I want to leave. I want to bail. I glance at the door and then back at Joe's face. It's like he's waiting for it. Waiting for the moment when I take off. I fumble for another cigarette, but his hand drops over mine, stopping me.

"Tell me about last night," he whispers.

"I have an ex . . . Brent," I start, my voice shaking along with my hands. "He's the one who I drove home the night of the DUI. We weren't ever that serious. We fooled around when we were partying. I guess he was that guy for me, you know? Kathy would call him an enabler, but I was right there with him. I enabled him just as much."

A giant well of silence sits between us. I don't know how to keep going, but Joe's face is so open and understanding, looking up at me from his seat at the table.

"We weren't safe."

"Because you were driving drunk?"

I shake my head. "No. With sex. We weren't always safe. I got pregnant. That night—the night of the DUI—I told him about it. I wasn't sure he'd want to talk about it, but he's been pushing me and he came over last night. And yeah, he wants to talk about it, only I can't. Not with him. It's too hard."

"You're pregnant?" Joe says, and I slam my eyes shut to avoid the judgment. When I crack them open again, his face is still open. God. How can he even be like this?

"No. I lost the baby. When I hit the stop sign. I was only a couple of months along. I'd been drinking a lot. I don't know. Maybe it would've happened anyway. So yeah, I'm not pregnant."

"And how do you feel about that?"

I take a deep breath. I need a cigarette so much right now. I fumble for my box and light up. Two full drags later, still standing next to the small table, I say, "Relief. Fucking relief. I'm a horrible person, but I didn't want a baby. I was ready to go back to boxing. Jerry, the owner of the gym, he once said I had a shot at amateur boxing. And I was going to do it. I didn't care that it went against my parents' wishes. I didn't care that it would be hard. Jerry saw potential in me and I thought, yes, maybe I can have this after all. If I could just get sober. But then I found out I was pregnant and it was like it all got snatched away from me again. And I hated the baby for taking that away from me, as much as I hated my parents for it. So yes, I was relieved when I miscarried. I didn't want the mess of it. I didn't want to have to tell my parents or figure out if I had the stomach to go into some shitty Planned Parenthood office and have them vacuum me out, though I'm pretty sure that's what Brent thinks I did. I didn't want to deal. And there's a part of me that wonders if maybe I didn't slam into that stop sign on purpose."

He nods. "You're not a horrible person."

"Joe. I just told you I'm glad my baby died. I get that you're tolerant, but for fuck's sake, let's not pretend this is okay. Let's not pretend I'm not a huge asshole for this one."

"I'm not here to judge you. You're doing enough of that on your own."

"Then what are you here for?"

He shrugs. "I'm here to listen. I'm here to tell you it's going to be okay. You're going to be okay. That you aren't the only alcoholic who has done or thought horrible things."

He stands up so he's right in my space. He takes the ciga-rette from my hand and puts it out in the ashtray. Then he wraps his arms around me and again whispers, "It's going to be okay."

And that's when I really lose it.

Chapter
Twenty-One

I'm not sure how long I stand there sniffling into Joe's shirt. Long enough to get it pretty damp with tears, long enough to smell all the parts of him: cigarettes, soap, laundry detergent, Joe. When I finally pull away I notice his eyes are wet with tears too.

"Why are you crying?"

He gives me a half grin. "Don't know. Guess I'm just hurting for you. For all of us. For what we all lost."

"You mean like a baby?"

He shakes his head. "No. Like a life. Addiction changes everything. And getting over it, getting through it, it involves constantly being on guard. And you're so young. I hate that this is your life now."

I step back from him. "I did it to myself."

"You did. And I'm glad you know it. That's a big part of the Fifth Step. But also part of it is knowing you're not alone. Knowing that you have this community of people who are right there with you. Who've all had moments where they've done something terrible. Your life isn't over now. There's still potential."

"Will you tell me now?" I ask in a low voice.

"Tell you what?"

"Tell me what your rock bottom was. Did you even have one? A real one?"

"Yours is real, Natalie, whether you think it is or not."

"Maybe."

"Natalie . . ."

I shrug. "You really want to know what keeps me sober right now? That was your question, right? Why I don't let sobriety go even though it's really fucking hard?"

"Yes. That was my question."

"You. You and Kathy and your relentless nagging."

He laughs, but it's a sad laugh. "Not the best idea to count on someone else for your sobriety."

I lift a shoulder. "It's what I've got. Now. What happened with you? You've got a rock bottom. Let's hear it."

He takes my hand and guides me back to the table. I consider lighting another cigarette, but I grab a pack of gum from my bag instead.

"You mean a rock bottom other than going to jail for driving into the White Hen and leaving the scene of the crime?"

"You told me you didn't get completely sober after you got out of jail."

He settles back in the chair across from me. "I didn't."

"So?"

"We're not done with your Fifth Step," he says.

"Yeah. But I'm exhausted after spilling the pregnancy news. And it's not much worse than that. I need a break. I need you to tell me when you were a huge asshole so I don't feel so bad."

He lets out a long breath. "You're not an asshole. It's not terrible not to want a baby at seventeen. It's not terrible to resent things in your life that keep you from your passion. It's not even terrible to let go of things that are hard. You could've handled it differently. Gotten help. But it's not—"

"Joe," I interrupt. "Please. My skin has been scrubbed raw here. I don't want to talk about it anymore. You need to give me something."

"Okay. Okay. My rock bottom. Well, when I got out of jail, I was going to meetings. It was part of my probation for a year. And I'd go to all the meetings, but nothing really sunk in ever. I'd go, get my card signed, then head back home and get wasted. I didn't drink with other people most of the time. I was too far gone for that. And I didn't want to get another DUI. So I was mostly home by myself."

I pull out another piece of gum and shove it in my mouth, my jaw aching at the extra work. My jaw aches a lot these days. I should probably give up the gum, but I have no idea what I'd replace it with.

"But this one time, I went out with friends. It was for

a bachelor party for a buddy. It involved this drinking game called Golf. Basically, every bar along the way is another hole and each one has a par. So the first bar the par was two beers. The second bar the par was a shot and a beer. The third was an upside-down margarita. Each bar had a specialty drink so that was usually the par. As you can imagine, by the seventh bar we were all really hammered."

I smile. "I can't believe you made it to seven. I probably would've stayed at the first hole and gone for a triple bogey."

He laughs. "I probably should've. Anyways, somewhere along the way, we picked up this hooker."

"Of course you did," I say with a smirk.

Joe raises his eyebrow. "You're judging me?"

I shake my head. "Go on."

"She started playing Golf with us, drinking just as much. In between rounds, she'd pull one of the guys into the bathroom for a quick blow. By the tenth round, I knew I should go home. Sleep it off. I could barely stand. I'm surprised any of the bouncers were letting us in."

"Yeah. Me too."

"The tenth round was tequila body shots. We were in the back room of the bar. No one could really see us. The hooker ended up in nothing but her thong underwear with all of us doing the body shots off her. I'm not really sure what happened after that."

I release a shaky breath. My whole body has gone tense.

Joe's telling has gotten cold and methodical. There's no warmth in his voice. Like he's told this story before to a less-friendly audience. On instinct I reach out and grab his hand. He squeezes mine for a second, but then pulls back. I spit out my gum and shove in a new piece.

"Someone must have sent me home in a cab. I was a blackout drunk so I lost a big chunk of the night. I've been told I made it to the fourteenth hole. I have no idea how any of the rest of the guys made it that far. Maybe they stopped drinking earlier. Anyway . . . I woke up the next afternoon with my head pounding and a dead hooker next to me."

The last part he says so softly I'm not sure I heard him right. "The hooker was dead? Are you kidding?"

He shakes his head. "Alcohol poisoning. I don't know if she came home with me and we drank more. I don't know if it was the rounds of Golf. I . . ."

"Jesus. I can't imagine. What did you do?"

"I called my brother," he whispers. "I called him and asked him for help. He had no reason to help me. None. I'd been an asshole to him and my parents before they died. I was a selfish prick and had absolutely nothing to offer but a dead girl and a tangle of problems. But my brother came. He called the police. He sorted it all out. Took me back to our parents' place, which we'd been trying to sell for a year. Shut me in there with him, stayed with me for a month, while I dried out, while all the pieces of me fell apart, while I searched through every cabinet and damn near killed myself drinking anything with alcohol in it, trying to forget that I was responsible for the death of a girl."

I grab his hand again. "You didn't force those drinks down her throat."

He shrugs. "I know. I've worked through it with my sponsor. I get that the choice was hers. But that doesn't change the fact that I was part of her death and I don't remember it. It doesn't change the night sweats I get sometimes, waking up with the image of her cold, lifeless body next to mine.

"Dead bodies in real life are horrible. We'd both pissed the sheets at some point in the middle of that night. Her skirt was hiked up and her panties were somewhere on the floor. We might've had sex. I don't know."

My hands are shaking. I spit my gum out and grab my cigarettes. I don't know what to say. My lost baby seems like nothing now. And yet it's everything. It's my connection to Joe. Someone else might be disgusted by him. Mom wouldn't be able to stay in the same room with him. But in my core I understand something about the two of us. Something no one else in my life does.

"That hooker could've been me."

Joe nods, swipes my cigarette from me, and takes a deep drag.

"The only difference is I woke up," I continue.

He nods again. "It could've been any of us, Nat."

"I'm sorry," I whisper.

"Me too. So much." His cheeks are wet with tears now. Not the sobbing kind, the silent ones that remind you of who you are and what you've lost. I woke up with so many of those kinds of tears when I was in rehab. My counselors always asked, but I couldn't say anything.

I take the cigarette from him and put it out. Then I stand and come to his side, hooking my fingers around two of his.

"Natalie." His voice is a choked plea. For a second I wonder if I'm doing the wrong thing here. If this is old Natalie, falling back on what's easy for me, what I'm good at. But as I brush the tears from his cheeks, I know I'm right to do this. I want this and not just to be wanted. I want this because it's real. We're real. He needs this and so do I. And it's right.

"Please."

I tug him to standing and lead him into his bedroom. The bed is made, almost military-style tight, and I smile when I see it. These are the things he has control over and everything about his place proves how much that means to him.

I turn when he steps into the small space behind me. My hands aren't shaking anymore. They're sure and steady as I pull his shirt from his jeans and unbutton it before sliding it off his shoulders. The T-shirt follows and he hisses when my fingers trace over his bare chest.

"We shouldn't . . . ," he starts, but I put my fingers against his lips to stop him.

Then I go up on my tiptoes to kiss him. It's been a really

long time since I've kissed anyone sober, and Joe's mouth is soft and gentle. He tastes like cigarettes and breath mints, which is strange, but I'm not sure my breath is much better, and the way he opens slightly makes me think maybe he doesn't mind so much either. I nibble his lips, and then something changes and he makes a sound in the back of his throat before gripping my hips and driving his tongue into my mouth.

It's a seriously good make-out session and I feel like I could keep kissing him forever except for the itching want that is traveling all over my skin. My fingers skim down and I undo the button and zipper on his pants. Then before I can slide them off, his hands are pulling at my shirt, and we're chest to chest. His hair tickling my bare breasts. It's so different from Brent's body, which now seems so much like a boy's.

My breathing speeds up and the itching moves closer to the surface. My hands open and close into fists. It feels like the only thing keeping me on the ground right now is the bite of my nails into my palms. I haven't experienced a rush like this since the first time I got in the ring.

I want everything to go faster. I want to crawl out of my skin and find a place inside him. I want to cement the two of us together and never come back from it. As quick as I can, I yank off my jeans and pull him on top of me, hooking my feet behind his hips. His jeans are only half-off.

He reels back. "Slow down," he whispers. "It's okay."

I shake my head. "No. Please. I can't . . . I need you to . . ."

"I know. Jesus, Natalie. Natalie. Natalie." It's a prayer and a plea at once, and everything between us clicks into place.

He slips off the bed and reaches for the side table, pulling out a box of condoms. My skin is on fire and the bottom of my stomach feels so achy and empty, like I want to devour Joe until the emptiness isn't there anymore. He pushes his jeans off, then rolls the condom on. I want to growl in frustration. Brent would already be done with the whole thing by now. But no. This isn't Brent.

My body is trembling. Not with fear. Not with want. With something else. Joe sees it and slides on top of me, pressing me against the mattress so hard it's difficult to breathe at first.

"Please. Please. Please." I don't even know what I'm asking for. But something is crawling up inside of me, screaming to get out.

"Let go," he says.

I shake my head and he shifts on me more. He links his hands to mine and pulls my arms above my head, pinning them down. I hook my legs around him and press my heels into his back.

"Please. Joe. Please."

He swears and I feel tears on my cheek. I'm overwhelmed, complete emotional overload, and pretty soon I'm going to shut down. I know this feeling. I've had it so many times before. Only, normally, I've fought myself out of it or dulled it with vodka.

Joe kisses away the tears and nuzzles along my neck, keeping his hands locked with mine. I arch into him, but he pulls back again.

The itching is so bad now. And I'm babbling and begging and then he's kissing me softly and whispering to me and telling me it's okay, I'm okay. He unclasps his hands from mine and pins my wrists, watching my face the whole time. "Beautiful Natalie," he whispers over and over again.

Then he slowly slides inside me and I cry out, pushing against his hands until he releases my wrists and lets me wrap myself so tight around him there's no space between where he ends and I start. And finally, finally, the itching inside me cracks into pieces and reshapes itself into something that feels like it actually belongs.

Chapter
Twenty-Two

It's dark outside and we're in Joe's bed, half-naked, eating Chinese food out of the boxes. He's been painfully quiet since we both collapsed into each other, prying himself off me the minute I stopped trembling in his arms. The walls around his emotions are high and I don't have the first fricking clue how to scale them.

"What happened with your brother after you dried out for that month?"

Joe's gaze moves to the side. He's barely looked at me, either. "He made sure I was okay. Made sure I got the help I most needed. Then he said he was letting me go. That he couldn't keep taking care of me. It hurt too much to watch me piss it all away time after time."

"I'm sorry," I say, and reach out to rub his cheek. He flinches and draws away. What. The. Hell?

He drags his hand over his beard stubble and says, "It gave me a weird kind of incentive, though, him letting go like that. I was sort of determined not to mess up again so he didn't have to dig me out of it. I promised myself never to ask him for anything again."

"So you haven't talked to him since?" I know the answer to this before he even says it. Joe doesn't know anything about what's going on with Kathy. He hasn't talked to his brother.

"No. Maybe one day. But for now I respect his wishes. He did a lot for me. Part of making amends with people is allowing them the choice not to forgive you."

So he's back in AA program mode. Like nothing happened here. Half of me wants to put my clothes on and blow the whole thing off, but the other half wants him to man the fuck up and either ask me to leave or take me back to bed.

"Do you think people are less willing to forgive you after you've screwed them over a bunch of times? Like maybe there's a limit and after enough times of you messing things up with them, they give up?"

He shrugs. "Don't know. Depends on them."

I nod and think about Camille. How she probably would forgive me because she didn't see the worst of me. I think about Brent. I don't know what to say to him or if he could forgive me. I think about Jerry and wonder if there's a chance of ever walking back into the gym and apologizing. If I'm strong enough for that. I nibble my lower lip and Joe stops me with a swipe of his thumb. Then achingly slow, as if he can't help it, he pulls me forward to kiss him.

Yes. He's still with me. Or at least part of him is. He's a really great kisser and I feel like I could spend days exploring his mouth, but a knock on his door jolts me backward.

"Natalie?" Mom's voice calls, sort of frantic.

"Natalie, get out here now." Dad, solid, unrelenting, brittle.

"Fuck. How did they find me?" I whisper, and snatch my jeans from the floor. Joe is already two steps ahead of me, tugging on his pants and T-shirt, mumbling under his breath.

This is going to be awkward. There's no two ways about it. Even if we don't look like we've been doing exactly what we've been doing.

The door rattles from Dad's pounding and Joe swears again and goes to answer it, barefoot. I try to tame my crazy curls, but it's no use. My hair, my face, my clothes, every part of me looks like I've spent the last three hours in bed.

I follow Joe as he tugs open the door. Dad is in a fury. His face is purply-red and there's a little spittle on the corner of his mouth as if he's been yelling. From my mom's face, I'm guessing he's been yelling at her.

"This is Joe," I say softly. "He's in the program with me. These are my parents, Tom and Sarah."

Joe holds out his hand, but neither of them shake it. Mom's in shock. Her eyes are wide and she keeps opening and closing her mouth like a codfish.

"Get your stuff, young lady," Dad says.

I shake my head. "We're having dinner. I did my Fifth Step with Joe. I'll be home later."

"Do not try that crap on me, Natalie. Do you know the state your mother's been in since you left? No calls. No texts. Just you disappearing after last night's vodka bender. It's a damn good thing I put the GPS tracker on your car or she'd still be home pacing. Have you checked your phone at all?"

"No. I turned it off. Doing the Fifth Step—"

Dad swats my words away. "Is that what the *kids* are calling it these days?"

I gasp.

Dad steps into Joe's trailer and pokes him in the chest. "You do realize she's seventeen? A minor. I have every right to charge you with statutory rape."

A choked sound escapes my throat. "Dad," I whisper. "He didn't rape me."

"Enough," he snarls. "I don't want to hear anything from you." Then he turns back to Joe. "And you're never to see my daughter again. Find another meeting place. Don't call her. Don't reach out to her. If you get near her, I'll slap an order of protection on you."

Mom releases a sobbing breath. She's curled into herself, wrapping her arms around her stomach like she's in pain.

I should say something to Dad. Say something to Joe. Do something to make things better. But I don't have any idea what to do to make Dad's anger dissipate. This is too damn hard and I feel myself shutting down.

Dad grabs my arm and tugs me toward the door. "We'll follow you in your car."

I look back at Joe. His face has gone pale and he's staring at his feet, taking long slow breaths. "Can I just have a second with him?" I say to Dad.

"No. You're done with this," Dad snaps. Then he pushes me out the door and says to Joe, "You're a disgusting shame of a man, preying on young vulnerable girls. How can you even live with yourself?"

Joe doesn't look up, but the tension in his body is so obvious. I want to wrap my arms around him. I want to whisper to him it'll be okay, but he shuts the door on us and I'm pushed toward my car, feeling more hopeless than I ever have in my life.

Dad takes my phone and sends me to my room the minute I get home. The shock of what happened at the trailer has worn off and now I'm itching to reach out to Joe and make sure he's all right. I'm not just going to roll over. This means too much and I'm past that now. Past avoiding things because they're too hard.

But without my phone, I'm sunk. Then I remember Joe's business card has an email address on it, so I pull it out of my wallet and power up my computer.

But Dad has disabled the Wi-Fi. Of fucking course. Jesus.

It's the worst kind of lockdown. I can't even call Kathy. I feel like I'm going to barf. The craziness of the past twenty-four hours is pinging around my head and I can't seem to grab onto a thought. The only weird thing is that I don't want to drink. Maybe because I realize it won't help me figure out how to fix the situation with my parents and Joe.

There's a light knock at my door and I know it's Mom before she even sticks her head in. Her face is more composed now, but she looks really sad. A small tinge of guilt pricks the back of my neck. I shake it off and put my hands on my hips.

"A GPS tracker on my car?" I say.

"Your father said it would help. It would give us the security of knowing we could find you if you relapsed."

"The Breathalyzer is supposed to keep me from relapsing."

She nods. "Yes. But who's to say once you get to a place, you don't start drinking? School starts back up tomorrow, Natalie. I was worried."

I shrug. "I was fine."

"You were drunk last night. Your moods are so out of whack. You've always been impulsive, swinging high and low, but since you got out of rehab it's like there's no telling what we're going to get with you. Maybe you're bipolar? Maybe we should let Dr. Warner prescribe something for you."

"Now? After everything? What was all that crap about kids being overmedicated and needing to learn how to deal with stress naturally? Suddenly you want Dr. Warner to get involved?"

She looks down. "I'm at a loss here, Natalie. I don't have any more cards to play."

I huff. "I'm not bipolar. I'm an alcoholic trying to give up drinking. I'm a girl who's spent her life trying to avoid difficult things in whatever way I can and now I realize it's not possible. Things are hard, that's life. I'm sorry if it isn't convenient for you that I'm suddenly getting my act together, but it's a hell of a lot better than me going on a Jack Daniel's binge."

She sits down next to me on the bed and makes a face when she smells me. I'm sure I smell like cigarettes, sex, and Joe. "What were you thinking, Natalie? Why would you get involved with someone so much older?"

I sigh. "He's good to me, Mom. He listens. He gets me. He doesn't want anything from me. He doesn't make me feel like I'm there only to make him feel good. He's real. He just—"

"He's twice your age. What am I supposed to think? This isn't making good choices."

"It is. I mean, I know it's unusual, but I like him. And he likes me. It might be hard, but we could work and he's worth it. It's not like older guys haven't been with young girls before. Look at George Clooney."

"Oh, Natalie, don't bring celebrities into this. That's hardly a lifestyle you want to model."

"I really like him, Mom." Feeling the truth of this again nearly knocks me over. I don't like him because he likes me or because it's easy, I like him for him. For how we are together.

She shakes her head. "You're not thinking straight. You're vulnerable right now. I know the program suggests not getting involved with someone until you're one year sober."

"Did you see that in a movie?"

Her mouth pinches. "Am I wrong?"

I sigh. "You need to talk to Dad. I can't lose Joe. I won't sleep with him again, but I need him as a friend. Please."

"You have a sponsor."

I grab her forearm and squeeze. "I need Joe. He's the only real friend I have right now. You have no idea all the things he's done for me."

Mom pats my hand. "You start back at school tomorrow. You should get some sleep. It's been a long day."

"Will you do one thing for me at least?"

"What?"

"Will you get Dad off the statutory rape thing? I don't want Joe stressing about that. There's no way to even prove we had sex anyways."

She flinches when I say the word "sex" but I need her help on this one. Dad is a dog with a bone when it comes to his decisions. It's practically impossible to talk him out of something, and my only hope is that his threat was just talk, not something he'd actually consider.

"Get some sleep," she says in answer. "We'll talk more in the morning."

Then, because she doesn't know what else to do, she pulls

the covers up and helps me slide beneath them. I'm still in my jeans and T-shirt, but I don't say anything. I let her tuck me in, kiss my forehead, and slip quietly from the room. My mind is racing but my body is heavy, and before I can figure out what to do, I drop into a deep sleep.

Chapter
Twenty-Three

I walk into school the next day, after a tense breakfast with my mom, and search out Amy and Amanda. They're both at Amy's locker, sipping from their water bottles. Amanda is sitting on the floor, back against the locker next to Amy's, with her legs stretched out.

"Give me your phone," I tell Amanda.

She looks up at me. "Where's yours?"

"My dad took it. I need yours."

The two of them exchange a glance. Amanda shakes her head. "So you only come around when you need something from us?"

"Yes."

"Well, then no. Go ask for help from your new sober pals."

I snatch her bag and rifle through it for her phone. I shove the bag back at her. "How many times did I sneak you past your mom? Don't be a bitch. You owe me."

"Whatever."

"I'll be back with it in a few minutes," I say.

I head down the hall to the newspaper office. It's usually empty in the morning, with all the journalism nerds waiting until after school to geek out together. I slip in and shut the door behind me.

I pull out Joe's card and punch in his number. It takes him four rings to answer.

"Yo," he says, and with just that one word, I know he's drunk. "Who's this?"

"You're drunk. Jesus, Joe."

"Ah. Natalie. You're not supposed to call. Statutory rape." His words are slurred, but I can make them out well enough.

"Where are you?"

"Not your business. We're done." There's a strange tremble in his voice and I wonder if he's maybe been crying too.

"Joe. Listen. I talked to my mom. It's going to be okay. We'll figure it out."

"No. Your dad's right. I never should've . . ."

There's a beat of silence while I'm thinking what to say. What can make this better. How to sober him up. "Joe . . ."

Then before I can come up with anything, he hangs up on me. I dial him back but it goes straight to voice mail. I try two more times. Finally I text him.

This is Amanda's phone. I don't have mine. Don't do anything stupid. Call your sponsor. I'll figure this out.

Of course he doesn't respond. I don't expect him to. I don't have any idea how far gone he is, but if he's drunk this early, I'm guessing it started sometime last night.

The first bell rings and I know I should get Amanda's phone back to her, but it feels like a lifeline. I fish through my purse and find the AA pocket guide. Kathy's cell number is scribbled inside. I take a deep breath and call her. It goes straight to voice mail so I leave a message.

"It's Nat. Things are shitty. I don't have my phone. You need to find Joe. He's in bad shape and sounds pretty wasted. He shouldn't be driving. And he needs to call his sponsor. I've made a mess out of everything. I'll try to call you from home later."

My voice doesn't even sound like my own by the end of the message. My heart is cracking and I can't breathe right. I've done this to Joe. And I don't know how to undo it. I slump to the floor and press my face into my knees. Tears leak from my eyes for almost the entirety of first period as I go over the events of yesterday in my head. As I think of Joe's years of sobriety and how one stupid thing ruined that.

I want to be sorry for sleeping with him, but I'm not. That moment, when he held me and told me to let go, it was better than almost anything I've experienced. And not because it felt good, but because it felt right. Like Joe and I fit more perfectly than anyone I've ever been with. And I hate that my parents ruined that.

By the end of first period, I've pulled myself together enough to go to the rest of my classes. I don't talk to anyone. I pass Amanda her phone at lunch and then walk out of the cafeteria, past Camille and her questioning gaze, past Brent and his concerned face. I spend the rest of the period in the library. My mind keeps clinging to the things I have control over. And praying for the things I don't.

Brent finds me after school.

"Sorry . . . about showing up at your house drunk," he starts, but I wave him off.

"You had your reasons."

He pulls his hand through his hair and I zip up my coat to signal that we're not getting into this now. "The thing is, Nat . . . I mean, you didn't really ask me what I thought. You didn't let me even work through all of it. You just decided."

"You thought you were owed something?"

He shakes his head. "I thought I was owed the truth a little earlier. I mean, how long had you known? Long enough to know you didn't want it."

I shrug. "I can't do this right now. It's really a bad time. I get you've been trying to talk to me, and I know I owe it to you, but not now."

"Jesus, Natalie, what the hell do you think is more important than this?" He looks so sad I almost want to hug him. But that's completely ridiculous. It didn't happen to *him*.

"Brent, a lot is more important than this. This isn't even a thing anymore. It's not an issue, so I'm not sure why you're making it one."

He flinches and I feel horrible. I want to see it from his

perspective, but I honestly can't. Not with the shit storm brewing in my brain over Joe.

"Look. I gotta go. If you want to talk more about this, or whatever, I'll sit and listen, but not now. I need to deal with some other stuff first."

He looks at his feet for a second, then fixes his gaze back on me. "I've given you a lot of time already."

"I know. I need more. Just a little more. Please."

He steps forward and squeezes my shoulder. "Okay. But don't blow this off. The least you can do is listen."

I nod and then spin out of his grip and in the direction of the exit. I need out. I need to talk to Kathy. I need to find Joe.

I beeline home, and when I enter the front door, I'm surprised to find Kathy in my living room, having coffee with my mom.

"I was going to call you," I say.

She nods. "I know. I got your message. That's why I'm here."

I look at Mom, wondering if she's given Kathy the lowdown on what she and Dad stumbled onto yesterday, but she shakes her head at me so I guess not.

"I'm gonna need more cigarettes."

Mom frowns and opens her mouth to start on probably yet another anti-smoking lecture but Kathy cuts her off.

"I've got some. You want to go to the coffeehouse?" Kathy is already tugging on her coat and grabbing her bag. I like this about her. She knows that I don't want my mom hovering while I debrief the mess of last night.

"Yeah." I look at Mom. "Is that okay?"

"Of course. She's your sponsor," Mom says, waving me off. But I can see the tension in her face and I'm sure she's wondering if Joe will be part of this little outing. I'm hoping with everything I have that he actually will.

"I'll be home in a few hours," I say.

"Try to make it before your dad gets home from basketball." This is more of a warning than a request. Dad does a basketball league with a bunch of other aging traders on Monday nights. He's usually not home until eight thirty.

I nod and follow Kathy out the door and into her car.

"I don't know where Joe is," she says as soon as she starts the car. "He didn't answer his phone and he's not home. I called his sponsor. He's checking the bars."

"It's my fault."

Kathy shrugs. "You didn't force him to drink again. You didn't funnel booze down his throat. He made his choice."

"But it was because of me."

"Maybe. Still. It's not your responsibility. The people who hurt us, they aren't responsible for our drinking. That's all on us. Remember the Fourth Step? You can resent people all you want, but in the end, it's your problem how you deal with that resentment."

I nod. I get it and I don't at the same time. Yeah, I might not technically be responsible for Joe's drinking, but the fact is he'd be sober right now if I didn't go to his trailer yesterday.

"But I *did* hurt him," I whisper. "I didn't mean to."

"Wait till I get some more coffee before you tell me what happened. I had a hell of a night myself."

"Your ex?"

"Yeah." She sighs. "I should probably tell him Joe slipped."

"Don't. Joe wouldn't want you to. He thinks he's put too much on his brother already."

Her face drops into a frown. "There's not a limit on love from your family."

"Of course there is."

She looks at me sideways. "Do you really think that? That if you push too much or ask for too much, your family will suddenly withhold love? That's not how it works."

"Yeah. It really is."

"No, Nat, it really isn't. Your family might be done with enabling you, but they're never done loving you. Robert, my ex, Joe's brother, he'd want to know if something was wrong with Joe. And he's a good enough guy that he'd even try to help. No matter what Joe wanted."

"Joe doesn't want to be a burden on his brother."

Kathy pulls over to the side of the road. She shuts off the car and stares at me. I look out the window at the fat flakes of snow that are just starting to fall. "Are we talking about Joe or you here?" she asks.

"Joe. Me. You. It doesn't matter. It's the same for all of us. We're burdens on our family."

"Everyone's a burden sometimes. Even when you're not a drunk. People get old and they need their kids to shovel the sidewalks for them. They get sick and they need someone to make them soup. When we're babies we need our parents to wipe our butts and feed us. When we're teenagers, we need our parents to bail us out of DUIs and send us to rehab." She smiles at me. "Or maybe just buy us trombones so we can be in the marching band. Whatever. It doesn't matter. There're going to be times when you're a burden. Just like there're going to be times when you're not. That's life. Your parents chose to have you."

I take a steady breath. She's wrong, I think. It's why I gave up boxing. Family can take love away. Everything is conditional. But I understand what she's trying to say and the partial truth of her words wiggles beneath my skin. Mom *does* love me, in her way. I mean, if that fucking elf didn't tip me off, I don't know what would.

"I slept with Joe," I blurt out.

"Ah." There's no judgment on her face, just a look of sadness. "Bad idea for you both."

"I'm sort of in love with him."

She raises a shoulder. "It happens. That's why they suggest sponsors of the same sex. Not that that means anything. But I don't think Bill W. was totally down with the gay community when he was drying out and coming up with his program, you know?" She starts the car back up again and pulls onto the road.

I blink at her. "'It happens'? That's all you're going to say? I tell you I love Joe and you tell me 'it happens'?"

She cracks her window and lights a cigarette. I light one too. "Of course it happens. We're addicts, Natalie. We glom on to things that make us feel good and don't let go. There's an entire section in the *Twelve and Twelve* about it."

I haven't gotten very far in reading the *Twelve Steps and Twelve Traditions* book, partly because I'm still baffled by the traditions and partly because I've been swamped with reading for school. Making up for that month in rehab is sort of killing me. Even if I'm not in super-hard classes.

"So you're saying I'm addicted to Joe now?"

She shrugs and takes another drag off her cigarette. "Maybe. He's a nice guy. He's been around for you. You've become sort of a project for him."

"Don't start with the project thing. I've heard it already."

"I don't know, Natalie. What do you want me to say? Being around him makes you feel good. I'm sure being around you makes him feel good. For most people this isn't a problem. But he's a lot older. How many teenagers do you know dating guys twice their age?"

"I'm not a typical teenager."

"That's right. You're more like an infant, learning to make good choices all over again. Learning that if you touch the oven, your hand is gonna burn."

"I'm not an infant. I know what I want. I'm clearheaded. I see what I'm getting into. I know it's going to be hard, but I want Joe."

She sighs and for a second I see all the exhaustion of years of battling addiction in her face. And a part of me says a prayer that I might have a different life than hers, which is cruel, but still. "Natalie. You're so young. So new to the program. All I'm saying is it's not uncommon for addicts to avoid dealing with their shit by replacing booze with a person. Getting wrapped up in love, lust, whatever, as a means to a different kind of high."

I puff on my cigarette for a few minutes in silence. I don't know what to say at first. I don't think Joe's an addiction like booze. And yet he is something I've held on to, needed even, when I wanted the shitty feelings inside to go away.

"By that logic, everything could be an addiction. Food, exercise, surfing the Internet, calling you, everything."

She nods. "That's right. And for you, you'll always need to be careful of that. Of becoming wrapped up in something to bypass your feelings."

"I'm full of feelings right now."

"Yes. But they're all about Joe. Or about you and Joe. The rest of it, all the things you should be addressing in your Fourth and Fifth Step, have now been cast aside for this thing. That's why they tell you not to get involved with someone until after a year of sobriety. Not because you aren't capable of a relationship with another person, but because you haven't established a solid relationship with yourself."

I shake my head. "This sounds a lot like therapy."

"Well . . ."

She tosses her cigarette out the window and I glance back at it. Joe would be pissed she didn't keep the butt.

"I don't want to lose him," I say.

"Me neither. So let's go see if we can find him."

We spend the next two hours scouring all the bars in town, then driving to his place to see if he's gone back home. He's nowhere, which means he's probably in the city and there'll be no finding him until he wants to be found.

I tell Kathy about my parents and the statutory rape thing. I looked it up at lunch and it turns out seventeen is the age of consent in Illinois. My dad's full of shit. She nods and tells me my family drama will pass. It's dismissive, but what else can I expect from her? She's not a guru. She's an alkie with her own shit, trying to give me a little of her wisdom. But our stories aren't the same. No matter what she says about me and Joe and becoming addicted to another person, I know different. We're right for each other. I just need to talk everyone else into it—including Joe.

Chapter
Twenty-Four

Joe is MIA for a week. Mom gives me my phone back on Wednesday, but he still won't pick up. Still won't answer my texts. I talk to Kathy every day. She's startled I'm not drinking, I think. I sort of am too. It's a battle every night. When everyone is sleeping and I know I could head to the CVS or Walgreens and get a pint. But I go down to the basement and work out instead. I'm already up to twenty minutes on the punching bag, four-minute drills with only thirty seconds of rest in between.

On Sunday I work the pancake breakfast with Kara by myself. We're slammed and even her usual peppiness is overshadowed by worry for Joe. Everyone asks where he is. I tell a partial truth—we can't find him, have you seen him?—but no one has seen him. He's part of this community, and everyone is worried.

Dad doesn't say one word to me all week. Neither does

anyone at school except Camille. She talks to me like an acquaintance and I know she wants me to somehow recommit to her, but I can't. I don't think there's enough in me to give her anything worthy of a real friend right now. Brent nods in the hall, but he's waiting for me to come to him and I can't yet. With everyone else . . . well, I'm sort of a ghost. I'm not sure how this has happened, but it's like stripping me of my party girl identity has made me pretty much invisible. Except to Mrs. Hunt.

"Two of your assignments received zeros because they weren't uploaded correctly," she says to me as I'm walking out after class on Monday. Her hair is tight against her head in a bun and she's wearing a pantsuit. She's like every Disney high school teen show cliché of a bad teacher.

"What? I did them right."

"You did not. The instructions were very specific about margins and spacing and you disregarded them. If you checked your assignments online, you'd know you received zeros."

"There was nothing about spacing on those assignments."

Her mouth drops into a frown. "There was. The instructions were very clear. I'm sorry you didn't take the time to read them."

The smug look on her face presses a button in me, and everything from the past week unleashes. An unstoppable wave of fury. My hands come up in fists.

"You. Fucking. Bitch. Are you kidding me? Your class is such bullshit. I did the assignments. I got extra time and I did them. Before any other assignment for any class. Because you were riding me so hard about it. Fuck you and your zeros."

I want to punch her in the face. I want to claw her eyes out. Instead I drop my hands and spit at her feet. She smiles at me. And it's awful and I know what's coming but I don't fucking care.

"You just earned yourself a three-day suspension. You'll receive zeros for the assignments on those days too. And lucky you, you'll be in really good shape to fail my class and have to take it again in the summer."

She points me to the door and leads me to the main office. Rage is bubbling over and my hands are clenched so hard I'm pretty sure I'm going to draw blood on my palm with my nails. I clamp my mouth shut and try to focus on my breathing. I've never been so angry in my life.

The entire time Mom is talking to the principal, I sit boiling in hate and say nothing. Mom pleads but apparently she's played all her sympathy cards and the principal is pissed. I receive a three-day suspension and have to write an apology letter to Mrs. Hunt.

On my way out of school, I see Brent. He eyes me and my puckered-mouth mom.

"Everything okay?" he says.

"Depends who you ask," I answer, my voice still sharp and full of rage. Mom stiffens next to me.

"Did you . . . ?" Brent starts, taking a step closer, but Mom slips in front of me.

"This isn't a good time, Brent. Thank you for your concern. Natalie will see you later." Then she grips my arm and drags me toward the exit. I don't even look back to see Brent's face.

We drive home in a silent car, and when we arrive, Mom takes my phone again.

"I'll try to keep this incident from your father," she says in a tight voice.

I shrug. I don't give a shit. He can go fuck himself. I pace my room for hours. Kathy calls at dinnertime—the home phone since I don't have mine—but I don't want to talk to her. It's not just Mrs. Hunt, who I frankly don't give two shits about, it's everything. I miss Joe with an unexpected ache worse than anything I've ever felt. Worse even than when I gave up Jerry and the gym.

I don't even have the patience to go online. I'm sure it's shut down anyway. Finally I lie on top of my covers and fall into a restless sleep.

I'm woken by arguing.

"We can't keep coddling her," Dad says. "She's seventeen. We've spoiled her and all this acting out needs to stop."

"She's hurting," Mom answers.

"Bullshit. She doesn't know what to do with herself. She's had it too easy for too long. She needs to start pulling her weight or leave."

"What do you mean 'pulling her weight'? She's our daughter, not a soldier. She needs our love."

"She needs tough love. When she's done with this community service, she needs a job and some discipline. I have a colleague who has sent his kids to work for the Youth Conservation Corps every summer and says it has been an invaluable experience."

Mom gasps so loud I can hear it through the walls. "You want to send her away? Even before college? That's a terrible idea. She's just getting sober. She needs us now more than ever. I don't even think she should go away to school next year."

"I can't have her in this house another year, Sarah. We need some semblance of a life back. There are expectations at work. I can't keep dodging parties and bowing out of obligations because I'm worried about my daughter's choices."

"That's a horrible thing to say," Mom snaps. It's a voice I rarely hear from her. She's a pleaser and she generally can carefully maneuver Dad into agreeing with her. Or she rolls over and lets him have his way. But now she's all venom and spite. "She's your daughter, not an inconvenience that keeps you from cocktail parties. She needs us. She needs *you*."

"Jesus Christ. What more do you want from me? I've broken my back for this family."

"Fuck you, Tom. Fuck. You. Everything you've ever done is for yourself. Stop pretending you're a saint. You think Natalie or I care about your money? You were the only one who wanted it. Wanted this life. All I wanted was a family."

Dad mumbles something, but it's too low for me to hear. Then a door slams and Mom starts crying. I should go to her.

Should try to comfort her like she's always trying to comfort me. But there's nothing I can do. I'm a disappointment to her, a misshapen piece that doesn't fit quite right in the puzzle. It would be best for all of us if I found a way out.

In the morning, I don't even pretend I didn't hear anything from last night. I grab a cup of coffee and sit across from Mom at the kitchen table.

"You okay?" I ask.

She nods. "Yeah. It'll be fine."

"You were pretty loud."

"I was pretty mad."

I laugh at this and Mom joins me for a second. "You going to be okay?"

"Did you lash out at Mrs. Hunt because of Joe?"

I take a gulp of coffee. "I don't know. Sort of. She's a bitch."

Mom shakes her head. "You spit on her, Natalie."

"Well, technically, I spit at her feet. If it wasn't going to matter either way, I should've thought to spit in her face."

"No. You would've been expelled. You never used to be this angry."

I lift a shoulder. "I was a fighter before. You don't get angry when you box. You have a place to put it all."

There's a long pause and I think maybe the conversation is done, but when I stand, Mom puts her hand on my wrist and tugs me back down.

"Do you hate us?" she asks.

"For what?"

"Keeping you from boxing."

"You didn't want it for me. It was my choice to give it up."

"But we pressured you. If I had known . . . Well, it doesn't matter. Hindsight is twenty-twenty."

"It's not terrible to be angry sometimes," I say, and I'm speaking for her as much as me.

"I know. But not about things you can't control."

I snort. "Mom. Look at you. Working the program."

She smiles, but it's a little sad. "Your father won't go after Joe. But you can't be with him. Not permanently. Not if you want to live in this house."

I don't want to argue about this. She's wrong, but she wouldn't understand my logic. She has no idea what it's like to need something so desperately. "I have to see him, though. To make sure he's okay."

"Natalie. I can probably talk your father into the boxing. If you really want it, but this . . ."

Mom's not stupid. She knows I'm close enough to eighteen to be able to do whatever I want. And for all that she is, she doesn't want to lose me by pushing me away. So yeah, maybe I suck for taking advantage of her, but I don't give a shit. I need Joe.

"Mom. Please. I have to see him."

She stares at me, then slowly nods. "Okay. Go see him. But that's it. Find a way to say good-bye."

There's no way in hell I'm doing that. But at least she's offering enough of a green light for me to formulate a plan. "I'm going to get dressed. He'll be home now."

I have no idea if this is true, but he's got to be home sometime. And I've got a three-day vacation on my hands.

"I'll drive you over," Mom says.

"No. Mom. I won't do anything. I just need to talk to him. You need to trust me."

It's a huge fucking ask. I know it is. I've hardly proven myself trustworthy. But still, it's Joe, and I have to see him. Alone.

"Be home by three o'clock. No exceptions. I don't want to regret this."

Relief spills over me, and out of nowhere I lean forward and hug my mom. She hugs back, too tight, too long, but it's like she's putting everything into that hug. And it feels like something real has passed between us, and for the first time in a really long time, I think our relationship will be okay.

Chapter
Twenty-Five

The only thing I can think to do is set up camp on Joe's front steps. I sit there for two hours, smoking cigarettes and thinking what I want to say. Mom made me wear extra layers and my long down coat, and I'm glad for it now. It's fucking freezing. Two and a half hours in and I'm considering going out to hunt bars, when his truck pulls up. Fucking finally.

Joe steps out and looks like he's aged a hundred years since I last saw him. But he's sober, thank God. He stops when he sees me, then plows forward toward his front door.

"Not today, Natalie," he says.

"I just want to talk," I whisper. I slide in behind him as he fumbles his key, shoving it too hard into the lock.

"No," he says. But he doesn't stop me from following when he pushes the door open and goes in. "I'm exhausted. I can't do this right now."

"Let me . . ." I don't say any more. Just take the keys from his hand and put them on the table before guiding him to his room. He drops prone onto his bed and I pull his boots off. He smells like a mix of body odor and cigarettes and I hold my breath as I'm pulling his shirt and pants off and wrapping his comforter around him.

"You look wrecked. Where have you been?"

"Staying at my sponsor's, drying out."

"How many days were you out?"

He shrugs. "Three or four. Don't know. Blackout drunk, remember?"

I touch his hair, but he draws back, tugging the comforter up. "You're sober now, though."

"Yeah."

"Do you want some water? Or . . ."

"Don't need your help. Just need sleep," he mumbles, but then he lets me press a glass of water from his side table into his hand. As soon as he finishes the glass he shuts his eyes and I have nothing to do but wait.

I consider calling Mom when it becomes clear I won't be home by three, but I know her worry will add more guilt onto my shoulders and I can only deal with one thing at a time. I text Kathy instead.

Found Joe. With him now. He's been with his sponsor. He's sober, but exhausted.

Should I come over?

Give me some time. We need to work some stuff out. Can you call my mom?

What's he doing now?

Sleeping.

Fine. I'll call her. Text me when he's awake. And don't fuck this up.

For a second I'm breathless. The reality of the situation comes crashing down on me along with an almost unbearable weight of responsibility. This is the hard stuff and I'm diving in headfirst. And Kathy isn't intervening. She's letting me go. Letting me fix this. Trusting me.

I squeeze my eyes shut for a second and pray. Then I slip on top of the covers next to Joe and watch him sleep.

It's five o'clock by the time he wakes. I've dozed off a few times but always jolted awake when he shifted or made a noise. When he finally blinks his eyes open, he stares at me with such empty sadness I want to crack in half.

"You're not supposed to be here," he says, and pulls at one of my curls before tucking it behind my ear.

"I know."

"Should I be expecting the cops?"

I shake my head. "I'm seventeen. That's the age of consent in Illinois. My dad was just talking shit. I looked it up on the Internet at school."

He flinches. "Natalie. That's not the point."

"No. You're right. But even if it were possible, Mom wouldn't let Dad press charges. It was a stupid threat to keep you from being with me."

Joe rolls onto his back and stares at the ceiling. "He wasn't wrong."

I lift up on my elbows and tap his chest. "He was. He wouldn't understand us. He wouldn't understand what we have."

He sighs. "Natalie. You're so young."

"It's not about that and you know it. I've had just as much life experience as you."

He rolls over and faces me. "No, you haven't. You're just getting started. Yeah, you've probably experienced more than the average seventeen-year-old, but you've still got the safety net. You *need* the net."

I cup his cheek in my hand. "You can be my safety net."

He pulls away. "I can't. Look at me. I relapsed. I'm okay now, but I don't have years of sobriety anymore, I have days. You need your parents."

"No. I really don't. They haven't done nearly as much as you have for me these past few months."

"Because they're not alcoholics. That's not something to hold against them."

I sit up and he follows so both our feet are hanging off the side of his bed. I take his hand and he lets me, twining our fingers together. "Why'd you drink? I mean, after everything, after so many years of sobriety, did my dad's stupid threat really push you over the edge?"

He rakes the fingers from his free hand through his hair. He still smells like he needs a shower, but his face is clearer. "It's complicated."

I let that sit between us for long enough that he sighs again.

"About a year ago, there was a girl who came through the program a lot like you. A bit younger, but with the same kind of chip on her shoulder. Entitled, bratty, I liked her right away."

I laugh.

"She liked me too."

I freeze for a second and shut my eyes, releasing his hand. "Tell me you didn't sleep with her."

"What? No. It wasn't like that."

I open my eyes again. "Well, there's that at least."

He blinks at me. "Do you really think so little of me? Five minutes ago you were going on about how your parents don't understand *us* and now you're accusing me of sleeping with every young girl who I become friends with."

I flinch at the harshness of his words, but raise my chin anyway. "We're alcoholics, Joe. We don't always make the best choices."

He stares at me for a long moment. "Exactly. *We*. Are. Alcoholics. You said it. Finally acknowledged it, for real. We're alcoholics. And we *don't* make the best choices. Remember that, Natalie."

He's spun my words on me and I want to punch him. It's

infuriating how quick he is to give up on us, to give up on what could be something great. "So this girl . . ."

"Yeah, well, she was doing really well. She had a sponsor. She was working the steps and getting her life together. I don't think she had the kind of money you do. And her parents weren't so invested, but she was doing good."

"So what happened?"

"She disappeared. All of a sudden. Stopped coming to meetings. Stopped calling. Wouldn't return my texts. She dropped off the face of the earth."

"Jesus." I release a breath. "That sucks. What does that have to do with me, though? I'm right here. I'm not going anywhere."

"I looked for her a long time when she stopped coming around. Even went by her house, but her parents said she ran away. They'd filed a missing persons report and everything. But no one could find her."

"So do you think they were right? Do you think she ran away?"

"I don't really know," he says. "But I realized something then. And I'd almost forgotten it until I saw the look on your dad's face."

"What's that?"

"I realized I can't save people. I can't be an anchor for someone. I couldn't be that for her and I can't be that for you."

"I didn't ask you to save me."

He shakes his head. "All you do is ask. Everything you do

cries out in desperation to be saved. You said it yourself. I'm the reason you stay sober. I can't be that. Don't you see? I want to take care of you. I want to make all the bad shit go away. I want to protect you from this life, from your shitty friends, from your absent parents. I want to give you everything, make you happy again. But it's not my job."

"I never said you had to."

"And that's the problem, Natalie." He takes my hand in his again. "You never asked me to, but I did it anyway. I wanted to. Christ, I still want to. And I can't be that. Because if it keeps going like this and I lose you one day, just like I lost her, it'll tear me apart."

"You won't lose me," I whisper.

He stands up. "You can't promise that. Not how you are right now. You haven't even been sober for six months. You're young and you have so much life ahead of you. But you have a road you have to take and I can't take it with you."

I stand up and take a step closer to him. "I'm going to prove myself to you, Joe."

"You don't have to . . ."

"No." I hold up my hand. "You said what you think. That's fine. Don't believe in me. Don't believe in us. I can believe enough for both of us. It's hard as hell, but I'm not bailing. I'm not taking the easy way out. Not this time. I'm going to fight for us. Because this is right. Just don't give up completely. You're a few days sober. Good. It was a slip. That's it. Stay sober. Fucking show up to meetings. Be here. And wait for me."

"Natalie . . ."

I press a kiss on his mouth, but he doesn't return it. "I'll prove it to you," I whisper again. Then before he can say anything else, I gather my stuff and walk out his door, texting Kathy to come over. I take two deep breaths, open and close my fists, then I breathe into the Breathalyzer, start my car, and drive home.

Chapter
Twenty-Six

I'm standing in the center of the gym before anyone notices me. Josh puts down his weight bar and takes a step in my direction, but Jerry grumbles at him from the opposite side of the room and waves him off.

Jerry's steps are long, measured strides. My heart is hammering so much I barely register all the other activity in the gym. I take a deep breath and let it out slowly.

I speak before he can say anything. "A long time ago, you told me you thought I could make it. Do you still think I can?"

"You're out of shape and fatter," he says, but the look on his face is enough to make my heart drum faster.

"What will it take?"

"Gotta get back here every day."

I shake my head. "I have AA three times a week."

He shrugs. "Come in the mornings. This summer you'll need to be here four hours a day, minimum."

I nod. "I might have to get a job."

"Your mom seems like she'd be flexible."

"Yeah. Maybe. But not my dad. He wants me to work some conservation corps to build character."

Jerry huffs. "Boxing builds character. Talk to your mom again."

I look up at the fluorescent lights, shutting my eyes for just a second and listening to the sounds of the gym. The grunts and the flesh smacking against gloves and the dance of feet skipping rope. It's so familiar. I return my gaze to Jerry and say, "What if she doesn't go for it?"

His mouth dips in a frown. "Well, that's the thing, isn't it? You're going to need to decide what to do with that. You're eighteen soon. I was on my own at eighteen, but you're softer than me. I don't want problems with your parents. It's on you to decide how much you want it and how much it's worth."

I look past him at the two guys sparring in the ring. Two years ago I could've beat both of them.

"Do you think I was addicted to boxing?"

He laughs. "Probably. Doesn't mean you weren't good at it."

"I'm trying to work on balance."

He shrugs. "So don't come back." But it's there, even if he won't say it.

"I want to, though. I want this. I don't want to let this go. I never really did. I was afraid, I guess."

The smallest grin flashes on his face. "Well, what do you

know about that? Seems like you figured a few things out while you were gone."

"Yeah. Okay then," I say.

"Okay," he answers.

I turn on my heel to leave, but he rests a hand on my shoulder. This is very un-Jerry. He doesn't touch you unless he's trying to beat the shit out of you.

"You're here. You got your stuff?"

I nod.

"Well, then, you might as well suit up. Show Josh how much work he may have in store for him."

A weight lifts from inside me and I give him a wide grin. "Maybe it won't be so much."

He throws a punch and his fist stops in front of my face again. This time I don't flinch. "Yeah, it will be."

I lift my chin. "What do you mean? I didn't flinch."

He laughs. "Yeah, but you didn't duck, either." Then he points me to the locker room and heads in the opposite direction.

Sparring with Josh kicks my ass. It's not even funny. I'd gotten fit enough at one point that I barely even felt hits. Now I feel every jab like it's a needle being stabbed into my torso. Josh is relentless and Jerry screams at me the entire time I'm in the ring. By the end, I'm drenched and breathing so hard I can barely speak.

"You let your body go to shit," Jerry says.

I nod, but I haven't felt this light in a long time. My head is in one place and it's here. For the past hour nothing with my parents or Joe or Kathy or Brent or my loadie friends has entered my brain. It's just this. Me, Josh, boxing gloves, and the rush of knowing that this might still be mine.

I grin before responding, "I can get it back. I'm not that bad off."

Jerry shakes his head, but I see a small smile before he looks down to unlace my gloves. "It's going to take a lot of work."

"Yep."

"You know what you gotta do, kid."

I nod and snatch my gloves from him, tucking them beneath my arm as I head toward the locker room. "I'll see you, Jerry. Thanks, Josh. I'll get you back soon."

Josh smiles and waves. "You better."

And I pretend I don't hear Jerry say, "Hope she's got it together this time," to Josh as I push through the locker room door.

When I get in my car I take a deep breath and hold on to the rush of fighting for another few seconds. Then I puff into the Breathalyzer and drive to Brent's house. His mom waves me in, her hard, assessing look turning to surprise when she sees me fresh-faced and sober. I've hardly made the best impression on her in the past, and even if she is cool with Brent, it sucks to be the girl a guy's parents want you to avoid.

Brent blinks in shock when he sees me and it takes him a

second to fully open his bedroom door to invite me in. I sit on his unmade bed and look at my hands, picking at the tape residue on my knuckles. Finally I feel him sit beside me.

"You wanted to talk?" I say, and I'm grateful my voice is solid.

"Huh. Thought you'd keep avoiding me."

I look at him now and I wonder if I'm ready for this. "Sorry, I just don't know what to say."

"Maybe that you got an abortion without asking me to help or how I felt about it?"

"So you *do* think that's what happened. I figured as much."

"Isn't it?"

I swallow. I do not want to have to explain this. "I miscarried after the accident. I mean, yeah, I would've probably gotten an abortion. I said as much at the party, but it didn't work out that way."

"Why didn't you tell me? I wanted to visit you in the hospital." His voice is painfully soft and I feel like donning armor. My hands ball into fists and a little tension eases.

"Yeah, but you didn't visit. And I didn't tell you because it didn't really matter. Plus I was dealing with court and rehab, and Jesus, it wasn't that big a deal."

"Thing is, Nat, it was my baby too. And I get that it means more for girls or whatever, but still, it's like I wasn't even part of it. You didn't think to call me in the hospital after the accident? I mean, did I even cross your mind?"

"Did I cross yours?"

"You know you did. I would've . . ."

"You would've what?" I hold up my hand. "You know what? Forget it. Let's not. We weren't trying to get pregnant. We were stupid and drunk and we fucked up on using protection. I told you I didn't want it. Let's not pretend that this all wasn't a huge fucking blessing for both of us."

He stands up and starts pacing. "I don't know. I mean, yeah, I don't want to be a dad at eighteen, but Jesus, it doesn't mean I'm not messed up about it. I'm sorry I wasn't there when I should've been, but cut me some slack here."

He paces back and forth a few more times and I try hard to see things from his perspective. How little control he had over everything and how frustrating that probably was to him too. And it was a dick move for me to drop the pregnancy news on him when the two of us were halfway to shit-faced at a party.

"I'm sorry," I say, and this is pretty much all I'm going to be able to give him. The baby, the accident, it's all too much and I don't want to have to do my Fifth Step with Brent, too.

He drops to his knees and takes my hands. "I'm sorry too. I fucked up. I should've come to see you in the hospital. I should've been more careful about condoms. But we were wasted and I don't even really remember when it happened."

"Me neither. That's kind of one of my problems. I don't remember a lot from when I'm drunk. And I do a lot of stupid shit."

Brent laughs, but it's sad and sort of pathetic. "Yeah, you do.

I mean, it was kind of funny sometimes, but sometimes it wasn't. And we were . . ."

"Not good for each other."

He brushes his thumb over my knuckles, circling around the red parts that don't hurt nearly as much as they did a half hour ago. "But you know, Nat, I like you. And not just the sex part." Now he blushes and looks down.

He's such a boy. Privileged and protected and a lot like me, or how I was a year ago. I brush my hand through his hair and it almost feels like petting a puppy.

"I can't be with you, B. It isn't the pregnancy and us always doing stupid shit together drunk. It's everything. I can't stand the idea that you've seen me be so terrible. It's too hard."

And now I understand Kathy's problem. Why she can't figure out what to do with her ex. Because it isn't him, it's her. It's having to live with someone who constantly reminds you of how much you once sucked. It's too much work. And in this case, letting go is the right thing to do.

"You won't even give us a chance? I mean, Jesus, why do you think I've been carting Amy and Amanda everywhere? They're *your* friends, and I'm trying not to be a dick and leave them to their own devices."

I stand up now and cross to the door. We're talking in circles and I don't want to keep going anymore. "You drink too, Brent. You're not a saint in all of this. And I never asked you to take on the A's full-time. That's not your job."

"Apart from that night I showed up at your house, I haven't had anything to drink in weeks. Did you know that? I don't need it. I don't care about it one way or another. I just mostly did it because that's what we all do . . . did, whatever."

"Then why are you hanging out with Amy and Amanda? You can't fix them. You can't fix me. It's not on you."

He rises and crosses to me. "I don't know. I feel responsible for them, I guess. If you won't let me be responsible for you, I can at least make sure they get home safely."

"Do yourself a favor. Drop the martyr complex. This is their problem. Driving them, taking care of them, it's all enabling. They have to sink or swim on their own, just like I did."

He folds his arms over his chest and looks smaller now. He's waiting and wants something, but I'm not sure what he expects from me.

"I would've helped you with the baby. Whatever you wanted . . ."

I snort. "B, you're eighteen. This whole conversation is too much for either of us. Drop it. I didn't and don't need the post-mortem from you, and we're both going to be fine. Really."

I swing his door open, but he snags my hand and squeezes. "I'll wait for you. I mean, we're friends and I'm around, so if you . . ."

"We're not going to be a thing. I told you," I say, shaking his hand off, and this time I'm pretty sure he gets the message loud and clear.

"I'll still be your friend, though," he says. "If you want. I'm not giving up on that."

I'm suddenly exhausted, the fight drained out of me, the need to patch up the pieces of my life too overwhelming in this moment. So I release a long breath and say, "I'll see you." And before he can say more, I escape the room to head back home.

Chapter
Twenty-Seven

I'm at the gym every morning and at AA three times a week. After that first time with Josh, Jerry hasn't let me spar. He says it's a privilege I have to earn back. He checks my court card when I walk in and then has me suit up for drills: jump rope, sprints, the bag. I've become a machine.

I eat lunch with Camille and her friends, but I haven't really opened up yet. She's noticed my bruised knuckles and asked about them so I told her I was boxing again. We're starting fresh as sort-of friends.

After the second week at her table, just as she's leaving, I mumble, "I'm sorry I let you go."

She stops, studies me for a long minute, then nods. "We let each other go. You pulled away, but I let you. I didn't think you wanted me around anymore. You had your boxing friends. Then your other friends." She gestures at the A's with both hands.

"You deserved better. Probably still do."

"We'll see," she says, then takes off as if we've resolved something. And maybe she has, but I'm still pretty lost when it comes to digging in with friends.

When I get home every day I talk to Kathy. I text Joe. He texts back but it's never much more than a soft dismissal. Cold but friendly. He doesn't go to meetings at SFC anymore. He's sober, Kathy told me, but I think he's wary of Dad showing up.

I haven't talked to my dad in two full weeks. He says something and I ignore him. He's tried getting angry, but it's in one ear, out the other with me, and he's at the point where he claims he's given up.

Poor Mom is the mediator. She talks between us, trying not to take sides, but there's no hope for it. I'm honest with her. I tell her how I feel. I tell her about anger and resentment. And finally, after years of avoiding the hard stuff, one day she cracks.

"Are you going to talk to me about the baby ever?" she says as I'm jumping rope in the basement. I stumble.

"You actually want to know?" I know she knows. There's no way she couldn't. Hospitals are pretty quick with medical bills, and there's no way she'd have missed a DNC. But I'm surprised she really is asking, addressing something head-on.

"Oh, Natalie, of course I want to know."

I sit down on the weight bench. "How come it took you this long to say something?"

She sits beside me. She stays here with me when I train, which is weird, but also sort of okay. I think it's her way of showing support. Since Dad is never around, it doesn't seem to have impacted him either way, though I'm not totally sure he even knows I'm back at the gym. She might be reaching out more with me, but she's gotten almost frosty with him.

It's less than six weeks until I'm eighteen and I'm guessing Dad's been counting down the time.

"Well, your dad doesn't really feel like we should discuss it. And I thought I'd let you come to me with it. But you haven't."

"Why would I? That's not our way."

She gnaws on her lip. "Maybe it should be our way."

"Are you mad?"

"That you had sex and weren't careful? Yes. But I'm not mad that I'm not going to be a grandmother."

A strange noise comes from the back of my throat. "You always wanted a bigger family," I blurt out.

"Not at the expense of my seventeen-year-old daughter living her life. Don't be ridiculous. Why didn't you tell me when you found out?"

I bark out a laugh. "Because I was at the bottom of a bottle of Everclear."

She pats my hand. "You're not now. And you still haven't said anything. I thought you were working on being honest. That's been . . . refreshing."

I shrug. "Well, you typically avoid the really hard things. And even with my new honesty thing, it's not always easy coming forward with more reasons for you to be disappointed in me. The smoking and the meetings and the DUI are enough."

She takes both my hands in hers. "Listen. You need to stop thinking like that. I know we haven't been the best parents. I know we've set difficult expectations for you. God knows we took away something that actually meant something to you." She waves her hand toward the punching bag.

"I get that you want the best for me . . . ," I start.

She shakes her head. "Yes, and there's where we went wrong. We decided we'd set the course for what was best without taking you into account. As if you didn't know what was best for yourself."

I look at our hands and let out a long breath. "I want to box. I want Joe. These things are what's best for me."

"Oh, Natalie . . . God, I wish I could make this easier for you. I wish I had a crystal ball so you could really see what this relationship with Joe could mean. It's not just the alcoholic thing. It's everything. How do you have a family with someone who is so much older than you? You don't know how hard it is caring for infants. By the time you're ready, he'll be in his fifties."

"Maybe I don't want to have a family. Maybe I want to box and live in his trailer and have this be my life."

Tears trail down her cheeks and I shake her hands off so I can brush them away. "I don't want that life for you, Nattie. I want you to be happy, but I can't see you being happy with that in the long run."

"You're doing it again, Mom. You're deciding what's best for me. When I'm eighteen, you'll have no say."

She smiles a little. "I have no say now. We both know this. But, honey, please, think long and hard about this. You have so many choices in front of you. Even if you want to box, you'll want to go to college eventually. Are you going to let go of living in the dorms with your friends to live with Joe? Are you going to skip parties and dances and all the rest of it?"

"Mom." I take a deep breath. I should be more used to this by now. "I'm an alcoholic. It's not the best idea for me to be going to those things anyway."

She pats my cheek. "Yes. You're an alcoholic. Already everything is going to be harder for you. Do you really want to take this on?"

I nod. "Yes. I love him."

She stands up and crosses the room. It's a strange departure and I can't tell if she's angry until she turns back and I see a mountain of sorrow on her shoulders. "Think about it, Natalie. I will love you no matter what. But that life will never be an easy one for you."

"Maybe easy isn't always what is right."

She nods. "Maybe." There's a long pause, then she says, "If you want to talk about the pregnancy ever, I'm here. I'll listen. I won't judge."

"Thanks," I whisper, but I know I won't be able to have that conversation with her. It's too loaded.

When I get done with my workout, I go upstairs to text Joe. It's something I've been thinking about for a while and I'm ready to ask him now.

I turn eighteen next month. Will you have dinner with me?

I hold my breath, but he doesn't text back right away. He has his phone. Joe always has his phone. Which means he's deciding. I jump in the shower and take a long time washing my hair. When I finally get pruney, I hop out and check my phone again.

Okay.

Chapter
Twenty-Eight

My dad is standing in front of the door, trying to bar me from going to dinner with Joe.

"Absolutely not. Not if you want to ever enter this house again."

I stomp to the closet and grab my gym bag. "Okay. Your choice. I'll stay at the gym."

"You're being ridiculous, Natalie. I know what's going on and I've let the boxing thing slide because it's keeping you sober, but you're not to go out with that man."

I glance at Mom, but her lips are pressed together in a thin line. "I'm eighteen," I say as calmly as I can.

"You're still a dependent. You're in high school."

I shrug. "I can get my GED. I can live at the gym. I'm eighteen. All bets are off here, Dad. It's time for you to make the call about how much you want to keep me as your daughter."

I've practiced this with Kathy. Last Sunday and every day this week over the phone. I've known it was coming. She's said I might be nuts but she's withholding any final judgment since she's moving back in with her ex and is hardly one to talk about potential bad choices. Joe has had a few brief conversations with his brother, according to Kathy, but things are still tense between them.

"You don't get to give me an ultimatum," Dad says.

"You're right. And I'm not. I'm giving you a choice. I am going to dinner with Joe. That is *my* choice for my birthday. You can respond to that any way you want. I hope you'll let me back in tonight. But I can't control that. I love you, Dad, but whatever mistakes you're trying to keep me from, they're mine to make. They've always been mine to make."

Mom gives me a little nod, but she doesn't say anything. She hasn't mentioned Joe again since that night in the basement. She's been to the gym a few times, even watched me spar without flinching or doing that Mom shouting thing. She's in a strange place of trying to reconfigure what we are to each other. And it's been sort of okay working it out with her.

"My choice is for you to go back to your room this instant and forget about this dinner," Dad says.

"That wasn't an option for you. That's out of your control."

"Oh, Jesus Christ. Enough with all the AA platitudes. I'll control what I want. You are *my* daughter. This is *my* house. I paid for the car you're about to leave in."

I pull my key ring out and slide the car key off of it. "Actually, Joe's coming to get me. You can have the car back."

His mouth drops open. "I'll call the police if he steps one foot on my property."

"And say what? That's he's taking your completely legal daughter out for dinner? Good luck with that, Dad."

Before he can argue more, say anything more hurtful, I push past him and walk out the door. He screams my name but thankfully doesn't come after me. When I glance back, I see Mom's hand on his arm, tugging him inside. I walk to the end of our driveway and take deep breaths as I wait for Joe.

It's been way too long since I've seen him. I know I look a little different. I've been working hard at the gym and my old body is almost back. I've earned myself a place in the sparring ring twice a week; the other days I'm building muscle, speed, power. I wore a dress even though my legs are freezing because I wanted Joe to see me at my best.

By the time he pulls up, my heart is dancing in my chest.

"Nice legs," he says as he pops out and comes around my side to open the door for me.

"Thanks," I say, and actually blush, like an idiot. There's a small gift on my seat and I shake it when he slips back into the truck. "Too small for cigarettes."

He nods. "Yeah. I heard you were off those with the training. Good for you."

"Yep. My lungs are super grateful. And I'm almost at a six-minute mile."

"Impressive."

He smiles and a lump forms in my throat. "I've missed you, Joe."

"Happy birthday, Natalie."

I tear open the packaging and pull out a box. "This looks an awful lot like jewelry."

He glances forward and raises a shoulder. "Yeah. Well. It's something like that."

My breath is coming in shallow bursts, and it feels like I'm in round two of a pretty intense fight. My hands shake as I open the box. It's a necklace with a three-month AA coin on it.

"I know you're still a few days away. But I got this one early. I'm proud of you."

I fasten the necklace on and touch the lettering on the coin with my thumb. *To thine own self be true.* I lean to kiss him and he turns so I just get his cheek. "Thanks," I whisper, and sit back.

He pulls his truck onto the road and heads toward town. "Where are we going?" he asks after a too-long, too-awkward silence.

"Where do you think?" I grin when he looks at me. "Red Lobster."

He laughs and all the strangeness of a few moments ago disappears. And I think maybe we can be us again. I reach for his hand and he lets me take it. He squeezes and I squeeze back.

"I got a job offer," he says after a few minutes of comfortable silence.

"Oh yeah? Another contract? Around here?"

"No. To go work for someone else."

I drop his hand because his voice sounds funny and a big warning gong is going off in my head. "That doesn't seem like it's your style."

"It might be a good change."

He pulls off the highway ramp and a million questions are bouncing around my head. But I force myself to ask the most important one. "Is it around here then?"

He turns into the Red Lobster lot and parks before he answers me. He clenches the wheel and finally says, "No, Natalie. It's in the Philippines. They're rebuilding a lot of houses out there after the typhoon. Lots of aid money has been poured into the country and they want to do more eco-friendly building."

My mouth drops open. "The Philippines? For real?"

He nods.

"For how long?"

"A year, maybe more. It depends."

"But you didn't give me a chance. You didn't give us a chance."

He gets out of the truck and comes around to my side. "There can't be an us."

I shake my head. "Yes. There can. I'm three months sober. And you're sober. And I'm boxing and I'm going to graduate because my mom and Jerry rode my ass until I made everything up to Mrs. Hunt, and I swear to God we can be a real thing. We can."

"You're eighteen," he says.

"Exactly."

"You've got your whole life—"

"No. Don't say I've got my whole life ahead of me. Don't pretend you're a fucking old man. That is *not* how this is supposed to go. I want this. I want you. And I'm fighting for it. Now man the fuck up and tell me what you want."

He reaches for my face and cups my cheek and I think I've got him. I think he understands and that he's there with me and he thinks it'll be worth it. But then he says, "I want you to stay here while I go to the Philippines. I want you to box. I want you to go to college. I want you to be sober. I want you to have everything."

My heart pounds too fast, anger searing through me. "Everything but you, you fucking coward."

I push away from him and march into the restaurant. He doesn't follow and I'm actually glad of it. I pull out my phone and call my mom.

"Natalie. Are you okay?" Her voice sounds weird, sort of sad and frantic all at once.

"Yeah. I'm fine. I'm at the Red Lobster. Can you come get me?"

"Where's Joe?"

"The fucking Philippines."

"What?"

"Nothing. I'll explain when you get here. Just please come."

"I'll be there in fifteen minutes."

I hang up and go into the bathroom. My perfectly done hair

that took me forever to do, my cute dress, my makeup applied so careful so Joe wouldn't see the bruises on my face from fighting. It was all for nothing. I feel like my heart has been ripped out and stomped on. He never even fucking gave us a chance. The only other time I've felt remotely like this was when I showed up last year to the gym drunk and Jerry told me I was a waste of space and talent.

When I go back out to the parking lot, Joe is gone but Mom's car is pulling up. I see her anxious face and I burst into tears. She bolts out of her door as soon as the car stops and comes to wrap her arms around me. I'm a wreck, sobbing so hard, babbling and not making any sense. She smoothes her hand up and down my back, then leads me to the passenger seat.

By the time she gets in on her side, I've composed myself enough to say, "He didn't want me."

"Nonsense," she answers. "He wants you to be happy. That's why he let you go."

I shake my head, but I can't answer. I can only look out the window and feel myself shatter into a million pieces. We're almost home before Mom says anything else.

"I've asked your father to move out."

My head whips around. "What?"

She nods and now I see the tearstains on her cheeks, but also a spark of fire in her eyes. "It was time, Natalie. Way past time."

I mirror her nod. "Was it because of me?"

She shakes her head and I know she's telling the truth. "No.

It was because of me. Because of what I want. We're not on the same road anymore, he and I. You're going a different path and he thinks I'm going to follow him on his. But I won't. I'm done following. It's time to make my own path."

"I'm impressed," I say, and I mean it. "Do you have a game plan?"

She grins and it's like something very real has happened to her and I've sort of missed it over the past few months. Like I've been so focused on training and staying sober and catching up at school and wishing for Joe that I didn't see how Mom grew a spine. "Of course I do. I've been asked to run the holiday events for the village."

"What?" I almost choke on my laughter because of course, of course she has, and it's fucking perfect.

"Well, the village doesn't just do the Holiday Walk. They have summer events, a fall festival, and several sidewalk sales and art fairs. It's a big responsibility."

"Oh my God, Mom. I know. That's huge. I mean, really huge. I'm so proud of you."

She nods and beams. "It's a lot of work. I talked to your father about it and he was completely against it. But I think I'm ready to take it on. I'll have other staff at the Village Chamber of Commerce to help me, but I'll be in charge of it."

I squeeze her shoulder. "I'm really proud of you."

She nods and looks at the coin on my neck. "I'm really proud of you too, Natalie."

Chapter
Twenty-Nine

It's my first real fight since I've started boxing again and I'm nervous as hell. It doesn't mean anything, from a technical perspective, but it could get me noticed when they're looking at up-and-comers to profile in the amateur women's boxing league press. Which could mean a whole shitload of good things for Jerry and me and the gym. I've got a new passbook from USA Boxing, so I'm official, which suddenly feels like a way bigger deal than I ever imagined.

And I want that for me. I can say that now and kind of own it. Kathy's helped a lot. Helped me figure out that it's okay to have a dream, to believe in yourself, to expect more than a shit sandwich. In the same way that she's helped me realize it's okay to be disappointed when shitty things happen.

Mom's next to me, awkwardly trying to massage my shoulders before Jerry shoos her away. Dad has been in his own apartment for a few weeks. He asked me to dinner last week, which was fucking excruciating and more a lecture than anything else, but I went and stood up for myself and told him I wouldn't see him again if it was going to be the same old crap. I owned up to the things I screwed up and waited for him to own up to his shit, but he didn't. Typical. I don't have a lot of hope for us, but it's Tenth Step stuff and I'm trying to believe it'll get better.

I'm legit at the Eleventh Step now, and I guess I'm proud of myself. In the same way I'm proud of my boxing. I'm cut, lean, and solid, and I don't even give a shit who at school says something about it. Even Mrs. Hunt is being nice—well, nice-ish. She paired me up for a class project with a basketball player named Troy who actually did half the work for our oral report. So now I either have lunch with Camille and her friends or I sit with the basketball players, and even though they sometimes make pricky comments about girls, they think it's cool that I fight and don't give me crap about it. Yesterday, for the first time, I let Brent sit with us too. He mostly talked to the guys, but I got it and was grateful for it because we're probably going to be okay.

My basketball friends are in the audience tonight; so are Camille and two of her friends, along with Kathy, and my mom, and Kara from the pancake breakfasts. My community service hours finished two weeks ago, but I'm still helping because Kara can't fucking figure out syrup to save her life.

The ref signals me and this Hispanic girl named Silvia to the center of the ring and gives us a spiel about a clean fight and how long the rounds last. I bump gloves with her and then I'm in my corner waiting for the bell and it's like everything I've been working so hard for comes down to this moment.

The bell rings and it's a shot to the heart. I feel like I don't weigh anything, and I'm out in the ring dancing on my feet and it's amazing. My fists are moving so fast Silvia can't land a solid punch because I'm lighter than air and she can't touch me.

Every punch hits its mark and she is crunched up and her guard is down and within three rounds it's over. Jerry is pounding me on my back and my mom is screaming in the best kind of way because it's not fear, it's total excitement. And even Kara is on her feet applauding me, though she looks totally confused, and I wave at everyone, then look for Kathy, who is farther down the bench. But my breath freezes in my lungs because next to her is Joe. A sob bursts from me and I want to claw through the crowd to get to him. He's smiling and I'm smiling. And Jesus, there is no better moment in the world than this one.

After I shower and hug my mom and thank everyone for coming, I go outside to find Joe. God, please let him fucking be here. I scan the parking lot and he's standing by his truck. I race over to him and leap into his arms. He oomphs when he catches me because, I've forgotten, I'm solid now. Strong and packed with muscles, so I'm heavier than I look.

"You came," I breathe, and hug him tight.

He laughs and hugs me back, then puts me down. "I did.

Kathy told me about it. You were amazing. You are amazing."

I grin. "I can't believe you came."

He smiles. "I wanted to see you."

My heart is a hummingbird. I'm almost light-headed with how good it feels to be like this, here with him. How good his voice sounds and his face looks. How much I want to slide into him and fit the two of us together all over again.

My grin breaks into a high-beam version. "I hope you aren't repelled by my fighting. I mean, not every guy would be into a girl who could kick his ass."

He nods. "True. But I'm not sure you could kick my ass."

I unzip my hoodie and show him my arms. "Have you seen these pipes? Did you see what I did to that girl in there?"

"Point taken."

The space between us shifts and he's staring so hard at my face I want to drop my gaze. I'm sure I have cuts and bruises. Not from Silvia, but from the sparring I did this week in preparation for this. But I keep my head high and let him drink me in the same way I'm doing to him. I count to ten in my mind and relax my breathing.

"So," I start. "You're here. And before I get too excited about what this means, I'm going to ask why you aren't in the Philippines."

His face goes expressionless. "I delayed my job. It wasn't a huge deal. There's so much work to be done, a few weeks won't matter."

Oh God. All the adrenaline from the past hour rushes out of me, pools at my feet, and leaves me feeling so hollow I'm not sure my heart's even beating anymore. Of. Fucking. Course. "So you're here to say good-bye."

He nods. "In a manner of speaking."

I feel like I've been punched harder than anything Silvia did to me in the ring. "Why fucking bother? You gave me your good-bye. Why would you even make me hope for anything but this?"

He shakes his head. "Because I didn't want to leave without telling you that I love you."

"You love me?"

He nods and I split open, my heart oozing too many emotions. I can barely breathe. God, why does this hurt so much?

"Yes, Natalie, I love you. And if things were different, I'd be taking you home right now. Every moment I was with you was a good one. I don't regret anything, except maybe telling you about the job too early on your birthday so neither of us got a chance to eat those Red Lobster biscuits."

I want to laugh, but I've got nothing. I think if a sound came from my throat right now, it would be like a bird dying.

"I want more for you, Natalie. I can't give you everything you deserve."

"No one can. That's not how love works," I manage to choke out.

"You could do anything, be anything. You don't need me."

"So you love me so much you're walking away. Again."

"Yes. That much. I love you *that* much, Natalie. And maybe one day you'll understand. And maybe one day you'll thank me. But I don't want to head out without that being clear between us."

I'm torn apart, broken into two pieces that don't feel like they'll ever manage to come together again. I want to fight and argue and scream and fuck. But none of it will matter. He's decided and there's nothing I can do.

"Good-bye, Joe," I say, because that's all that's left.

"Good-bye, Natalie. Make yourself a good life." He leans down and kisses me and it's so bittersweet that I almost choke from the sob escaping my lips.

Then he's in his truck and I'm standing in the parking lot with my bag of boxing gear at my feet and my heart right next to it. I look at my phone and send a quick text to my mom before getting in my car.

When I slide the key into the ignition, my phone rings. I'm sure it's Mom but it's actually Brent.

"Hey." My voice sounds shaky, but not terrible.

"Aw, shit. Did you lose?"

I swallow hard. "No. I won actually. In just a few rounds." I glance at my red knuckles and a surge of pride bumps up against the pain of Joe leaving.

"That's great. Congrats. Why do you sound like crap?"

I choke on a sob. "Not one to mince words, are you, B?"

He laughs. "Certainly not at this point."

"It's nothing. There was a guy. I thought we could have been something we're not."

The sharp inhale of his breath tells me he's still there, but he says nothing.

"Brent?"

"Yeah," he finally says. "Sorry. That took me by surprise. Didn't know you were seeing anyone."

The reality of it all hits me in the gut again and I blink back tears. "Well, it's complicated and we're not seeing each other anymore."

After another long pause, Brent says, "But you'll be okay, right? I mean . . ."

For the first time in months, I feel like having a cigarette. I reach for my bag, then forget that I got rid of all of them after Jerry made me jump rope for forty-five minutes straight.

"Will I be okay?" I echo. "I don't know. I guess. Love sucks. Even stupid, ridiculous, impossible love."

Brent laughs again. "Yeah, Nattie. It really does." His voice cracks and I shake the sound from my head like I'm shaking off a stinging jab.

I can't deal with any more of his sadness and I don't want to explain any more of mine, so I say good-bye and toss my phone back into my bag, my hands gripping and loosening on the steering wheel. It feels like my insides have been scooped out of me and all that's left is this hollow need. I glance at the clock, breathe into my Breathalyzer that Mom and I can't figure out how to disable, and start the car.

I'm late and have to sneak in the back, but I need this more than anything right now. I've missed the announcements but I know them anyway. It's full, but Friday nights always are. My knee is bouncing as I listen, and I don't even really know what I'm going to say, but I raise my hand.

"Hi, I'm Natalie. I'm an alcoholic."—"Hi, Natalie"—"I won a boxing fight tonight. And lost someone I love. Within fifteen minutes it went from being the best night of my life to the worst. And I guess that's how it goes sometimes. And I don't want to drink. Not really. But I want the hurt to go away. I wanted him to love me enough to risk it all, only he didn't. Or maybe he did. It still sucks, though. But I'm here, which I guess is something. And I'll go home to my mom and watch a bunch of shitty movies and maybe eat a pint of Ben & Jerry's and wake up tomorrow remembering everything, and hurting again. But sober. Thanks for being here for me. I guess I'll keep coming back."

Acknowledgments

This book wouldn't have been possible without the help of my dear friend Jay Asher, who is ragingly patient and tolerant of me. Thanks for sticking around, Asher, even when there were a lot of reasons not to.

To my formidable editor, Liesa Abrams, you are a very good partner for me and have given so much love and care to this book. There aren't enough words of gratitude.

To the entire Simon Pulse team, who has showered this book with support, particularly the cover artist, Dave Foster, and my adorable publicist Kelsey Dickson. Thank you, thank you, thank you.

To agent Jonathan Lyons at Curtis Brown, Ltd., who has been a champion of this book from the start. Thanks for seeing all the best things about it, J.

To Mandy Hubbard, who read the first fifty pages and suggested Nat have something she's passionate about. You said horseback riding and I went with boxing. Tomato-tomato, Mandy. It was still a great idea.

To my critique partners, Jolene and Lucy and Carrie. Your brains are astounding and I love how much you fill in the giant holes I manage to leave in my first drafts.

To Kristina Martin and Leslie Wu, thank you both for

directly and indirectly supplementing my amateur women's boxing knowledge.

To Drew, Ted, Carrie, Amy, and Gayle. You are a very good circle. I'm grateful for every email I exchange with the lot of you. Ted, I am particularly grateful for your invitation to come watch you box. I promise I'll get there one day.

To Brent and Bryson, the two of you really make my days way better. Thanks for believing in me.

I'm also extremely blessed to be part of the YA writing community at large, who fights and listens and tries to make things better every day. You have welcomed me and I'm so glad to be part of you.

Finally, a mountain of love and gratitude for my family and friends, who have stuck with me through everything. My parents and sister, who cheer and help with the kids and ask me about my books even when they aren't really your bag. My friends, who pull me away from my computer to do roller derby and eat sushi and go to book clubs and teach Sunday school and talk. I would be lost without you. And most of all, to my husband, Julio, you will always be my first, last, and everything. Jojo, Bijou, and Butter, you are the best parts of me. I'm so lucky to be your mom. I love you.

SDG.

Turn the page for a look
at another powerful
story from C. Desir.

BLEED LIKE ME

Their worst addiction is each other.

C. DESIR, author of *Fault Line*

I wasn't supposed to be born. My mom's doctors had told her over and over that severe endometrial scarring would make it practically impossible for her to carry a baby. But my infant self didn't care about scarring. Or the partial hysterectomy Mom had to get after my delivery. And for most of my childhood, we were happy in our little pod of three—Mom, Dad, me. Until my parents got a different notion about the magic number three: adopting three boys from Guatemala.

And I learned to disappear.

It was easier for everyone. I became the quiet one. The one who didn't drain my parents of everything they had. Pathetic as it might sound, going to school and working at the Standard Hardware were the good things in my life. When I wasn't there, I was tucked away in my bedroom, coming out only to referee arguments between Mom and my brothers when one of the neighbors called about the noise. Or to help when Mom gave me the ragged, desperate face she had on now as I stood at the open front door. Her gray roots were an inch thick at the crown of her head, and she was wearing the same outfit she slipped on every day after work: stained, discolored T-shirt, saggy sweatpants with too-loose elastic at the waist.

"Luis has locked himself in the bathroom again and Alex won't eat any of his snack until Luis comes out." Her exhausted voice passed through me. I'd heard it for almost five years, too long to even remember what the Mom of my childhood sounded like.

I dropped my messenger bag at my feet and opened the drawer of the small side table next to the overloaded coat-rack in the hall. I plucked one of the emergency hotel key cards from its box and took the stairs two at a time. My heavy boots squeaked on the scuffed hardwood. The loud explosions from Miguel's Call of Duty game echoed from the living room.

I pounded on the bathroom door at the top of the stairs. "Luis. Get out of there."

"Fuck off."

Jesus. What did the other fifth graders think of this kid? He spent more time in the guidance counselor's office than in his own classroom. But no amount of "be respectful and appropriate" lecturing from my parents or school officials made a dent in his colorful vocabulary.

I shimmied the card along the edge of the doorjamb, wiggling it into just the right spot. *Click.* I swung the door open. The bathroom was trashed. Toilet paper and shaving cream were everywhere. A bottle of cough syrup sat sideways on the sink, its contents spilled all over the toothpaste and toothbrushes. Not quite a childproof cap after all.

Luis stood with his arms crossed. Brown, unapologetic face, black eyes boring into me as if I were personally responsible for the crap state of his life. "That cunt won't let me play video games."

I squeezed my eyes shut. He'd trashed the bathroom over a video game? I shook my head. Mom didn't deserve this even if she did sign up for it. "Clean it up."

"Fuck off."

"Clean it up or I'll hide Alex's blankie."

His eyes flared in alarm and then burned in hatred. The kid didn't care one bit about himself, but threaten one of his brothers and he came out swinging. He snatched a washcloth from the drawer and dropped it onto the cough syrup mess. "I'm gonna get my brothers out of this shithole. Soon."

"I'm first," I mumbled.

"What?" he asked, pausing in his half-assed cleanup job. "What did you say?"

"Nothing."

I pointed to the washcloth and he started sopping up the mess again. His thin shoulders shook as he muttered curses. I called down the stairs to Mom, "He's out. Tell Alex he'll be there in five minutes."

"I need to go to the library to study," I said at dinner, pushing leftover spaghetti across my plastic plate.

Dinner was the worst time of the day. The "pretend we're a happy family" time where cell phones weren't allowed and we all had to announce two things we'd learned in school. Two. Things. Did my parents ever even go to high school?

Mom had become an expert in making every meal in under eighteen minutes. Eighteen minutes was the maximum allowable time she could leave the boys without chaos erupting. I had no idea how she'd figured this out statistically, but I trusted her on it and got used to dinners that came frozen in bags or popped out of the microwave. Family "together" time was loud boys barking orders at Mom.

My parents had adopted my brothers off the streets of Guatemala City when they were six, four, and three. They were only going to take one of them, but they could tell the brothers were bonded and they wanted to keep them as a unit. We'd had so many family discussions about the benefits of siblings. I was twelve then and just starting to get pissy about being the sole focus of my parents' relentless hovering. Mom stared at babies everywhere we went, then came home and gushed about how her sister had been her best friend growing up. The sister who'd moved to Germany and rarely called anymore. My dad said he'd always wanted brothers. They both promised it would change all our lives. It did, but not like any of us expected.

"I need to go to the library to study," I said again, between Luis's demands for more milk and Alex's complaints about how he got too many tomato chunks in his sauce.

"I need to go to the library to study." Repeating sentences three times gave me the best chance of them actually sinking in.

I hadn't been to the library since seventh grade. But I was testing out the ratio of success in getting away from my brothers. Good lies need to be tucked away for emergency use. Most people don't realize this and use them too frequently, so they're no longer effective. Big mistake.

"You can study here," Mom answered, the desperate "don't leave me with these monsters" look flashing across her face.

"It's too loud and—" Before I could finish, Luis snatched Miguel's dinner roll from his plate, and then Miguel punched him hard enough to make Luis squeal.

Cue sibling fistfight number three. A new record for family dinner.

I scraped my half-eaten spaghetti into the trash and ran upstairs while Mom pulled the boys apart. I glanced in the mirror: jeans, black T-shirt, hoodie, boots, stripy hair, chain necklaces, too-pale face, too-thin body. Still the same me. Sometimes I would squint when I looked in the mirror and imagine I was someone else living a different life, but the blur never lasted. The dinginess of my room and the hollowness of my eyes always broke the illusion.

My boots thunked on the stairs as I headed back down, grabbing my bag before returning to the kitchen. When I walked in, Mom was standing at the counter, dropping more dinner rolls onto a baking sheet and lecturing the boys about how they should just ask her to make more if they're still hungry.

"Okay, I'm going."

"Be back before ten." Mom waved at me and continued her lecture. Alex flashed his missing-tooth grin and then flipped me off as Mom turned away. Nice. Miguel and Luis were kicking each other under the kitchen table when I walked out. A crash followed by a shriek from Mom punctuated the door click behind me.

The skate park stayed open until eight on weeknights in September, closing for the season on October first. I walked to it on autopilot, having spent so many summer afternoons watching my brothers fly up and down the ramps. They bitched endlessly about the helmet requirement, but after two trips to the ER for stitches, they'd gotten the point about head injuries.

The night was cool and quiet. I parked myself on top of the high hill I normally sat on to watch the hard-core skaters practice. A chain-link fence surrounded the ramps, and on a clear night I could see the blinking lights of the Chicago skyline in the distance. I lit a menthol cigarette and blew rings of smoke toward the dusky sky. I shut my eyes and listened to the boards zipping down ramps and the low voices trash talking and laughing. Did my parents ever watch me at the skate park when I was younger? Before the boys and all the trouble? I couldn't remember.

"Skate girl, huh?" a voice broke into my cocoon, and I blinked the menthol buzz away. A tall, too-thin boy stood in front of me, smirking. A bright blue patch of hair dropped in front of his left eye, and a retro Sex Pistols shirt clung to his lanky frame.

"What?" I blinked again and shook my head.

He gave me a small smile and shrugged. His eyes traced over me, and it took everything I had not to cross my arms over my chest and move away.

"Why aren't you with the rest of the chain-smokers at the Punkin' Donuts?" he said. He took a step toward me, and I slid back so I could see him better. My eyes dropped to the aerosol can and paper bag he held.

"What are you doing with that?"

He sprayed the can into the bag and stuck his face into the fumes. His chest puffed out as he inhaled. I pressed my hand into the grass beneath me, plucking at the cool wetness. Wetness I could feel along the back of my jeans.

He coughed and dropped the bag to his side. "Livening up the evening."

I looked him over again. The rest of his hair was dark brown like his eyes. His jeans hung low on his hips, but not in the annoying way where they practically fall off. The bones of his shoulders jutted out from his shirt. He grinned at me, slightly dazed.

"Are you retarded?"

"Nope," he said, and the grin cocked up even higher on the side of his mouth not hidden by hair.

"You sure? No one huffs here. It's country."

"Country?" He shook the can again.

"Yeah, as in it's for idiots who can't find better drugs."

He chuckled, and I stared at the way his hair fell across his dark eyes and clear skin. No acne. How does this even happen to guys? He brushed his long fingers over his mouth, and I followed them as they fell back to his side. Hands have always been interesting to me, and his moved too gracefully in comparison to the rest of him. Like they didn't know they were on the end of a sloppy boy.

"Well," he said, dropping the can into the paper bag,

"huffing wouldn't be my first choice, but we're in the suburbs. Sometimes you gotta work with what you've got."

"We're like three El stops from Chicago. My grandmother could score drugs in this town."

He shrugged. "Maybe I like the fumes." I looked him over again. The thumb of his left hand hooked in his jean pocket while his other fingers drummed against the denim.

"Huh. My brothers huffed on the streets of Guatemala to keep from getting too hungry." Why'd I tell him that? Why was I even talking to him? Shit. Shit. Shit.

He took another half step toward me. "Yeah? Your brothers are from Guatemala?"

"Adopted."

"Obviously." He motioned to my pale face and blue eyes. Something was written on his palm. I squinted to see, but it was too blurred.

Enough. I stood up and grabbed my messenger bag. "Okay. Well, it was nice meeting you. I'm gonna go talk to some of the boarders."

"What's your name?" He reached out and fingered the hoops running up the side of my ear. I flinched and knocked his hand away. Goose bumps prickled along the back of my neck. It'd been too long since someone touched me.

I took a step around him. "Amelia Gannon. But no one calls me Amelia. It's just Gannon."

He pushed his hair off his face, and I saw a metal bar peeking from his eyebrow. "Gannon. Yeah, I like that."

"Glad you approve. I live to please. Really." I slid my pack of cigarettes into my pocket. I took a step to the side and he countered. People normally weren't this interested in having a conversation with me. I crossed my leg behind me and stared at him for an uncomfortable amount of time. "So?"

His eyes looked glazed, and it occurred to me his interest might be more from the fume high than anything else. It made sense. I wasn't exactly the kind of girl guys got in big conversations with, even random blue-haired boys with eyebrow piercings and nice hands.

"So what?" he said, reaching out to trace my hoops again.

"Dude, back off." I grabbed his wrist and dug my nails in. "Why are you touching me?"

He dropped his hand. "I like your hoops. They're sexy."

My cheeks heated, but I squinted my eyes at him. "Listen, whatever your name is, you can't just go around touching people. You'll get your ass handed to you."

He tilted his head back and laughed. His Adam's apple bobbed along his slender neck. I gulped as something warm pooled in my stomach. Shit.

"What are you doing here?" I asked. "Are you a boarder?"

He snorted. "Fuck, no. I was never sober enough to learn

when everyone else was figuring it out. Seems kind of stupid to try it now."

"You mean when everyone learned in, like, fifth grade? One of those child addicts, eh?"

His face froze for a half second, but then he grinned. "Something like that." He drummed his fingers on his jeans again. "So do you skate?"

"No. Not in a long time. Too busy working. I just come here for the amusement of watching guys fall on their asses."

He grinned. "One of those types, then?"

"What types?"

He looked me up and down, and my stomach knotted. "The angry girls."

My fingers tightened around the strap of my bag. "Not quite."

He leaned closer. "Then what type are you?"

"I'm not any type." I inched back. My strong instinct to bolt warred with the depressing realization that I had no place to go and the even sadder fact that this guy was the first guy in a long time to talk to me without asking for money or cigarettes.

"So where do you work?" he said, dropping to the grass and patting the spot next to him.

I didn't move. "Standard Hardware."

He patted the spot again. I stared at his fingers and tilted my head, trying to decide if he was being friendly or stalky. Chitchat wasn't my strong suit, so it was hard to say. He released a sigh before yanking me next to him. I scrambled to get up, but then his hand touched my side and I froze.

"Relax, Gannon. It's a nice night. I want to talk to you. You don't have to be so cagey."

I shifted away and narrowed my eyes. He offered me a goofy boy grin. I hugged my knees to my chest and focused on the boarders.

He grunted. "So a job at the hardware store must mean you know your way around tools?"

I couldn't help smiling. "Yeah. Pretty much."

His hands moved to the sleeve of my hoodie and he brushed away a piece of dried grass. His fingers lingered over the outside of my wrist before I snatched my hand away.

"I like girls who know their way around tools."

"Are you being gross?"

He laughed and nudged me with his elbow. "That's *your* head in the gutter, not mine."

"What did you say your name was?"

"Michael Brooks. But Brooks to you. Okay?"

I shrugged.

"So . . ."—he picked at a piece of loose string on the edge of my jeans—"do you want to hang out for a while?"

"Not really." I had nowhere to go, but I still wasn't sure

about Mr. Grabby Hands Brooks. Or my weird response to him.

He chuckled. "You don't like me?"

"You're a little handsy for my taste."

He laughed harder and pulled his hand back from the loose string. "Not normally. It must be something about you."

It was a line. It had to be. But why was I being singled out to be on the receiving end of cheesy lines? "What are you talking about? You just met me."

"I go to your school."

I stretched my legs out in front of me. "Since when?"

"Three weeks ago. Haven't you seen me?"

I turned to him and laughed in his face. "It's a big school. And why would I have noticed you?"

"I've seen you," he said, and shifted his knee so it touched mine. The warmth of his leg made me feel strange and, if I was being completely honest, a little bit good. "Come on. Let me walk you home."

"You're not walking me home. I'm not telling you where I live."

"Okay, I'll walk you somewhere else, then."

"Who even said I was leaving?"

He nodded to the flickering street lamp behind us. "Skate park's closing soon. What're your plans for the rest of the evening? Is there any place else you'd like to watch guys fall on their asses?"

I pulled my phone out of my messenger bag to check the time. It was too early to consider going home. My brothers would still be up.

"I think I'll stay here a little while longer."

He inched close enough that his whole thigh pressed fully against mine. "Me too, then."

I shrugged and tamped down the heat on my cheeks, grateful for the growing darkness. "Suit yourself." I held out my pack of cigarettes. "Want one?"

He scoffed. "Filtered menthols? I don't think so. I smoke real cigarettes."

I lit another cigarette and dropped my lighter into my pocket. Smoke curled around me, and wetness from the ground seeped further into the back of my pants. But the warmth of Brooks's too-close leg kept me from paying much attention to the cold discomfort. Neither of us said a word. I opened my mouth to ask what he was doing there in the first place, but somehow the question felt like an intrusion into the strange peace blanketing the night.